Author Diane Nielsen was born and raised in the Panhandle of southwestern Nebraska. She has been entertaining others with her stories since the age of nine.

Besides her passion for creative writing, Diane loves spending with her two sons, family, rock hunting and the Nebraska Cornhuskers.

This is Diane's fifth book and Finale in The Guardian Series.

Other Fictional Romantic Drama Books Published by Author Diane Nielsen are:

"WISH ME DEAD" Book #1 in The Guardian Series
"DARK WHISPERS" Book #2 in The Guardian Series
"DARK SECRETS" Book #3 in The Guardian Series
"OMEN LAKE" Book #4 in The Guardian Series

And last but not least:

"SILENCE" the Finale in The Guardian Series

The Finale in The Guardian Series

Diane Nielsen

Order this book online at www.trafford.com
or email orders@trafford.com

Most Trafford titles are also available at major online book retailers.

Print information available on the last page.

ISBN: 978-1-4907-8339-0 (sc)
ISBN: 978-1-4907-8338-3 (e)

Trafford rev. 07/18/2017

Trafford PUBLISHING® www.trafford.com
North America & international
toll-free: 1 888 232 4444 (USA & Canada)
fax: 812 355 4082

"SILENCE" – the fifth and final novel in The Guardian Series is dedicated to my parents Harvey and Mary Heilbrun. I am what I am today because of you! Love you both!!

And to Robert Goodwin Esq. for being a good friend to my dad and the whole family! Your kindness has definitely earned you heaven points!! Always know you are appreciated!!

Prologue

Saul heaved a tired sigh as he stood before the Window to the World and watched his human charges. From this place he could stand guard and, when a problem was detected, he could act quickly to prevent the Dark from getting their black claws into innocents as they tried to turn mortal souls from the paths that Destiny had written for them at birth.

Roman, the leader of the Dark, cracked the whip over his Minions' heads, commanding them to bring more to the Dark side. Even though their numbers were bloated and unimaginable, he wanted more. Always more!

Ever fighting this Dark tide left Saul tired, tired and weary all the way down to his bones. No matter how hard the Guardians fought it never seemed to be enough. No matter how many Dark Ones the Guardians put down ten more, a hundred more were waiting to take their places.

Saul stood alone and watched as mighty nations fell because the Dark Ones had been able to take over leaders of these great countries. He watched as the mortals were lead like sheep to the slaughter as these same leaders sugar coated their words of war. Making those they were entrusted to protect, swallow them and ask for more, while being blinded to the fact they were about to be sold out for some personal agenda.

There were special humans that could see through the masks of deceit that these dark souls wore. But keeping them alive and protected, as they fought to bring good back to humanity, was starting to look like a loosing battle.

Two such humans, Hannah and Dee Priest, each a favorite of Saul's and the loves of Guardian Hunter Jaxon Riley and Guardian Hunter Gunn had recently fallen, being claimed by the Omen Lake. Saul, Jaxon and Hunter had arrived just in time to pull their souls from the grey waters that tried to suck them down into the Dark. Saul was glad that both Jaxon and Hunter were reunited with their soul mates, but Hannah and Dee's deaths had given the Dark a stronger hold on mankind and, once again, the Guardians had to fight from a disadvantage.

Saul rubbed a hand across his face and sighed again. As he stood amidst the cool clouds he heard a whisper in his ear. "*What now?*" he thought, as he knew all too well that a call from the Fates could not be ignored.

Being the mightiest Immortal Guardian of them all earned Saul the honor of being able to converse with the Fates, and when they called he answered. He had no other choice.

"I am here," Saul said, as he appeared before the Fates and awaited their words.

"You look tired," the Fates whispered, concern for their champion evident in their collective tone.

"I am fine," Saul assured them, standing straighter and ruffling his wings in denial. "Why have you called me?"

"Another human is to be born," they said, their voices gentle as a breeze. "We need you, once again, to pick a soul to inhabit this human and watch over it as it grows and ages."

"Very well," Saul said, as his mind started to whirl. "I shall do as you ask."

"Thank you Saul," they said, before they departed. "You are, as ever and always, appreciated." And with that they withdrew.

Saul assumed this human was to be special since they called on him to fulfill their request. But he would have to take time and think before choosing a soul to be reborn.

"Saul," a small voice called. "Can I talk to you?" it asked and waited for his reply.

Saul nodded his head and waited as the spirit of a small child came to stand before him.

"Hello Leonard," he said. "How have you been?"

"I've come to ask you a favor," Leonard said, looking down at his feet. "I know I did wrong," Leonard began in his quiet young voice "when I wished for Ashton to join me. I know I acted badly and you had to fix my mistake as best you could. I know that my place as a Guardian and my wings had to be taken until I learned this and could again be trusted to protect those I was sent to guide."

"Go on," Saul gently encouraged when Leonard faltered.

"I was wondering, when would it be my turn to be reborn?" Leonard asked, scuffing a small toe through the air. "I have been training and learning all my lessons and my teachers are very pleased with me and well, I just wanted to know if you would please consider me the next time a baby was to be born. I promise you will be proud of me," he said, begging without pressure.

Saul looked at the small boy before him, at the dark curly hair that covered the boy's head, and reached out to lay his hand upon that same head. He felt the softness of that hair and he wondered if indeed this soul could be trusted. If this soul had indeed learned its lesson. Maybe it was time to trust Leonard and give him one more chance. After all, he was in need of a soul and he would be able to keep a close eye on him as he grew as a mortal.

"I don't think this is a good idea," Ashton said softly, coming to land behind Saul, her wings of deep red shining in the sun.

"Why not?" Saul asked the trusted Guardian, willing to hear her counsel.

"Just a feeling I have," Ashton admitted for Saul's ears alone. "I just have an uneasy feeling about this soul."

"Is it because of what he did to you in your last life?" Saul asked, arching a fine brow at his friend.

"I can't say," Ashton admitted, a frown creasing her beautiful brow. "I really don't know why, but I have this nagging feeling that if we let this one back on earth, something really bad is going to happen."

"Thank you," Saul said. "I will consider your advice." he replied before he watched Ashton take to the air and fly away.

Behind Saul's back, Leonard curled his small lip and stuck his tongue out at Ashton as she tried to persuade Saul to not let him go. He was bored with his existence and wanted to at least be able to live a human life. He could never get away with anything because that one, that Ashton, she was always watching, always spying and he hated it. He hated having to look over his shoulder and hated seeing her everywhere he went. Why he ever wanted her as his friend was beyond his comprehension. Because he was ever so sure he could do better. Much better!

Leonard's brown eyes began to burn with the hatred he had hidden for so long. But he stamped it down one more time as Saul faced him again.

Saul turned back to the small soul and stared until Leonard began to squirm under that stare.

"Very well," Saul said. "I will give you this one last chance to prove yourself. But should you fail you will not be allowed back with the Guardians. Your soul will be forced to move on and to where will be chosen for you."

"Thank you!" Leonard squealed, before jumping around like a hyper rabbit. "When can I leave?" He wanted to know, anxious to be out of this place.

Saul smiled at Leonard's enthusiasm and hoped he would not regret his decision. "I'll be watching," he said, as he passed a hand over the dark head and watched as Leonard faded away and was placed into the body of the baby waiting to be born.

"I'll be watching," Saul said again and vanished.

Roman rubbed his hands together, licked his lips and laughed.

He'd been watching too, and now it seemed his wait was finally over!

Show time!

Chapter 1

Ethan Goodwin opened his eyes slowly, blinked once and closed them again. *"Five more minutes"* he thought *"just five more minutes."* It was toasty under the heavy covers and he knew what waited for him after he got up, got dressed and started his day. Snow!

It was in the air yesterday, had been all day. Ethan could smell it as soon as he had walked out his back door. The wind had taken on a damp bite that drilled all the way down to a person's bones by late afternoon.

Snow meant extra work when you owned a ranch in Wyoming, but Ethan was used to it having been born and raised on this same ranch, the ranch that had been in his family for three generations and soon to be four.

He rolled over onto his side and gently draped an arm over his sleeping wife's bulging middle. His hand lightly caressed the hard mound and he felt the strong kick under his palm as he said a soft "good morning" to his son.

His son…he liked the sound of that. He smiled.

Matilda, Mattie, his wife and he had gotten married in their early twenties and had been trying for a child ever since. Now twenty years later they were finally going to get their wish.

It had been a shock to both of them when they received the news that they were pregnant, and both had shed tears of joy as they celebrated in the impersonal examining room at the doctor's office. A baby! They were going to have a baby!

Both had spent many hours decorating a room for their new son and it was finally finished. All that was missing was the new baby.

Ethan placed a light kiss on Mattie's shoulder, careful not to wake her. As her time grew near she had not been sleeping well. Being in her early forties, the strain on her body had left her tired and achy.

As the baby again stirred under his hand, he sent a thought to him telling him to let his momma sleep a little longer. The activity slowed and stilled, bringing a smile to his lips as he liked to think the little one had heard his request.

"Good boy" he whispered, and smoothed the taunt skin one more time before flipping back the covers and, as quiet as possible, got out of bed to begin his day.

He dressed, brushed his teeth and made coffee before dressing in warm layers and heading out the door.

Ethan had been right. Snow was falling in huge, heavy flakes sticking to the ground and covering the frozen dirt until only white could be seen. As far as the eye could see, only white.

He pulled on his gloves as he walked to the barn and the surrounding corrals to start the morning chores. He watched as the cows and their new calves found the bales of hay he cut and strung out and, with hunger, began to devour their meal. He made sure the heater was working on the water tank so the liquid stayed fluid throughout the day and he opened one of the barn doors so his babies could have shelter if the storm became rough.

This was the time of year that he calved out and he had to make sure they were born in the barn and did not drop on the cold unforgiving snow.

A couple of hours had passed before Ethan was satisfied that none of the expecting mothers were about to give birth and it would be safe to go back to the house to fill his own belly with a hot breakfast. Even though he had told Mattie many times that she did not have to be up cooking, she still had his food warm and ready when he walked in, shivering from the cold and knocking snow from his coat and hat.

He loved her so much it hurt when they were apart, so both made sure parting was only done when necessary. Maybe that was weird to some but that was the way they liked it.

Ethan hit the back porch and was puzzled to see their Saint Bernard, Gabriel, sitting down, leaning against the door with soft whines coming from his massive throat.

"Hey boy," he said, reaching out a hand and stroking the silky head "What's wrong?"

The huge dog wagged his tail, thumping the porch in greeting until it sounded like a base drum in a band, bringing a smile to his human's face.

"Let's go inside buddy," Ethan said, standing and turning the knob to the door. Gabriel pushed past him before the door was barely wide enough, ripping it out of Ethan's hand to bounce off the wall with a bang.

Ethan's heart began to beat fast and his breath caught in his throat. Something was wrong! Gabriel had always been protective of himself and Mattie, so when he felt the need to muscle his way in first Ethan paid attention.

Ethan pulled off his coat and hung it up before bending down and taking off his muddy, snow-covered boots.

"Hey Mattie!" he called, walking into the house. "What's up with Gabriel?"

He got no answer. Walking into the kitchen, he noticed that the table was set but there was no food to be seen.

"Mattie!" he called again, feeling another prickle of fear tighten his chest. "Mattie where are you?"

As he rounded the corner to the short hall leading to the back bathroom his heart skipped a beat and his mouth dried up.

On the floor lay his wife, on her side cradling her pregnant belly. Gabriel stood over her licking her face and whining in concern.

"Mattie!" Ethan yelled as he knelt by her side, trying to roll her onto her back without causing her pain.

Gabriel stepped back and let his human tend to his wife, never taking his eyes off the pair. That is until he sensed a presence enter the house and approach the pair on the floor at his feet.

The hair on his thick neck and down his broad shoulders stood up and, at once, his stance became defensive. His lips pulled back in an ugly snarl that bared inch long teeth and his eyes became black with anger.

"Stay back!" he growled to the dark shadow that had stopped just beyond his reach. "Stay back or I'll kill you!"

Roman pulled his black, wet lips back in a sneer that imitated the animal baring his way before moving back to a safer distance. He knew the dog could not hurt him but he also knew the Guardians listened to the animal protectors they placed with the humans they watched.

Roman could wait a few more hours. After all he had been waiting for years for this soul to be brought back. He could wait. And, with that, he faded from the Goodwin home, leaving Gabriel ready to die to protect the humans he loved.

Ashton appeared at his shoulder and laid a calming hand on his furry head.

"I heard you." she soothed "I heard you. Good boy, good boy!" she praised as Gabriel licked his lips and shook his head to calm down.

"I'm here now." she said, rising to her full height, spreading her immortal wings.

"It's my turn now." she said.

"It's my turn."

Chapter 2

Time was a blur and Ethan was soaking wet with cold sweat before he was finally able to point the nose of his pickup towards town and his final destination, Regan Memorial Hospital.

He had been so careful, lifting Mattie off the floor, supporting her until she could stand on her own. He mostly carried her until she was sitting in a padded chair at the table while he sped through the house collecting all the essential and planned for things needed when the time was right to head to the hospital and have their baby. And it did not take a rocket scientist to figure out that that time was now.

Ethan had forgotten a very important lesson his father had taught him when he was just a small boy tagging along with him as he did his daily chores. The lesson being that when a storm blew in at calving time, babies started hitting the ground in record numbers, along with the snow that piled up.

Ethan had not connected the dots, those being that Mattie's time was near and a major winter storm had been forecast and had indeed showed up with a vengeance.

He had prepared for his calves to arrive, but had missed preparing for his son to be born also.

"Stupid, stupid, stupid!" he chided himself as he warmed up the pick up, called his neighbor to check on his cows. Ethan loaded the bag to be taken to the hospital in the backseat, before pulling as close to the back door as possible and getting his wife and making her comfortable in the passenger seat.

He shut Gabriel in the back porch for protection from the storm, before slipping and sliding his way around the truck until he reached for the icy handle and climbed in himself.

"Are we ready?" he asked Mattie, squeezing her hand and trying to appear calm for her sake.

"I'm ready" Mattie said, a strained smile on her lips. Her beautiful sky blue eyes turned dark as another pain gripped her body.

"Let's go have a baby then!" Ethan said, putting the truck in gear and hitting the gas. The back tires screamed as they fought for traction where there was none. Ethan gritted his teeth as he flipped the vehicle into four wheel drive and inching slowly out of the driveway and onto the county road leading into town.

He wanted to stomp on the gas and get to the hospital fast, but the snow and ice had other ideas. Stepping on the gas accomplished nothing more than making the ass-end of the pick up creep sideways, threatening to send them into a spin that would land them in the ditch.

A couple of times Ethan was sure that was exactly what was going to happen, but each time the pickup righted itself and he kept its nose headed towards town.

"Ethan," Mattie warned after the last skid was corrected, "don't make me have this baby on the side of the road. I know you have tons of experience birthing calves, but if we have problems I don't want you to have to get the calf puller out to fix them".

Mattie mentally patted herself on the back because, just for a moment, the look of terror on her husband's face was replaced by the smile she had fallen in love with.

She didn't say so, but she needed Ethan to be strong. Strong for her because she knew that before long she was not going to be able to hold in the moans as the labor pains came faster. But, for now, she rode out each contraction in much fought for silence.

Ethan was not an idiot and he knew exactly what Mattie was doing. She was trying to put his mind at rest using humor. But he watched out of the corner of his eye and knew each time her fingers gripped and turned white with a new pain. And he knew her time was getting close.

Ashton rode in the back seat, monitoring Mattie's pain, marveling at the strength of this human as she carried each wave inside her, not letting on how badly she wanted to scream and cry out.

Ashton knew time was short and, at the rate they were going, arriving at the hospital for the birth was not going to happen unless she lent an unseen hand.

Leaning forward, the Guardian placed her hands on Mattie's shoulders, taking in the bulk of her pain until she was as comfortable as possible, then exiting to reappear at the back of the truck.

Ashton did not feel the bitter wind as it blew her long dark hair behind her, nor did she feel the icy spray of snow kicked up by the tires as they dug into the deepening drifts. The freezing metal of the tailgate did not burn her hands as she gripped it tight and drew down hard with her immortal wings giving speed to their travels. The vehicle did not swerve or skid because Ashton guided it along the road until the hospital was in sight. Even then she did not let up until Ethan slammed on the brakes at the Emergency Room doors.

Ashton stayed and kept watch as the new baby struggled to be born. And, with a smile of pure joy, she wiped a lone tear from her cheek as the first cry of the new human rang our clear and strong.

"I wish that could have been us." Sam whispered in her ear as he appeared to fold her into his strong arms.

"We would have had beautiful children." Ashton said into her soul mate's wide chest. "They would have been beautiful."

Sam could not reply because the lump of regret that clogged his throat left no room for words to escape. He could do nothing except wrap his own wings around his love and kiss the top of her head.

Sam slowly rocked Ashton as she mourned what could have been. But he did not mourn. Not any more. Instead he burned with anger at Leonard for having taken their mortal plans of destiny from them. Taking from them this precious moment Ethan and Mattie now shared.

"You're finished for now," Sam said, as he took Ashton's hand to lead her away. "Tomorrow is soon enough to begin watching over the boy."

Ashton looked one more time upon the newborn's face before allowing Sam to lead her away.

Sam knew that Ashton would watch over this mortal, even though Leonard's soul had been assigned to Saul to guide.

But neither Saul nor Ashton would know that he, Sam, would be watching too. Watching to make sure that history did not repeat itself, and there would be no chance for this being's soul to cause pain to anyone else ever again.

Surely, with all three of them keeping watch, destiny would have a chance to unfold for this human. But Sam had no idea what that destiny was. If he had, he might have taken the child's life, and sent the soul on its way, saving mankind the blackness that bloomed there.

But the child lived and, for this night, all was well.

All was well until the forces of Darkness had their way and chaos would reign like fire around this soul.

It had begun.

Chapter 3

Roman too visited the room, waiting until all was silent and the shadows were still, deep and black.

He paced at the end of the hospital bed, keeping his black eyes focused on the newborn that slept soundly at his mother's side. He watched as the father kept a protective arm draped over his sleeping wife and the other hand resting on his new son. "Like he would be able to protect them if I, Roman, decided to strike," he scoffed.

He felt the love and pride Ethan harbored for his family as it rolled off him in waves, and Roman wanted to gag at its goodness.

Roman knew this soul and had almost harvested it from the ranks of the Guardians once before. But Saul had found out his plan and had stepped in to save Leonard before he had been completely lost to the side of the Dark. Yes, Saul had taken Leonard's wings and had reduced him to a mere spirit. But Roman had been patient, waiting for his time to try again. And here it was.

Roman stilled as the baby cooed and opened its eyes, seeing nothing but the darkness that surrounded him.

A small fist waved in the air until it found its way to the mouth that instinctively opened like a hungry bird's with the first touch on its cheek.

Roman loomed over the baby, watching as it tried to feed off the fist that finally found its way into the tiny mouth, and he smiled. Reaching out a blackened stick-like finger, he pushed the tiny fist out of the way and let the baby suck the foul digit into its mouth, giggling as it swallowed the blackness from Roman's dark being.

Roman pulled the finger out of the hungry mouth, liking the small pop it gave as the boy was reluctant to let go, before touching the small chest with the same black jagged nail. Darkness seeped into the small chest and, as it did, a seed was planted in the pure, innocent human infant's heart. Roman would allow it to lay dormant until the time was ripe for him to nurture that seed and help it grow.

He bent down and peered closely at the baby, trying to figure out just what made him so special. If a gift of power had been bestowed upon him at birth, Roman could not see it, could not smell it. The only thing he could find that made it special was the fact that it had been born to a childless, middle-aged couple.

A twisted smile appeared on Roman's lips as an idea came to him.

"Tell you what," Roman whispered to the watchful baby. "I have a gift for you." and he again reached out a finger tip to touch the tiny chest.

"With this gift I claim you as mine!" Roman vowed as he implanted his Dark gift into the new being, watching as it wormed its way under the fragile skin until it was absorbed into the pure soul, until the dark, baby blue eyes turned as black as pitch.

"I give you the gift of darkness," Roman said, before twisting in glee at his own evil deed. "I give you the gift of causing the ones that care for you, and even call you friend, never ending pain."

Roman licked the dark hole he called his mouth, as drool hung in wet ropes from the black lips, before dropping onto the shiny floor and pooling there to smolder.

"Sleep!" he ordered the child when he had finished doing his happy dance. "But be ready to do my bidding when I command. For from this moment on you will secretly know me as Master and will do as I bid."

Satisfied with his work, Roman returned to the shadows until the morning sun chased him back to his dark abode. From there he could watch as the boy grew, and when he was ready he would unleash his monster.

Unleash him to cause nothing but PAIN!

He laughed!

Chapter 4

Mattie woke with the rising of the sun and, for just a moment, her heart beat hard as she remembered her dream. It was a bad dream in which something dark and very bad had threatened her son.

Her son. Just those words chased away the remainder of the dreams and allowed her heart to fill and overflow with the love she had been harboring for a child.

For so long Ethan and she had been trying to have a baby, but eventually they had given up hope of it ever happening. Then seven months ago they had received the news that they would soon be blessed with the most precious gift. The gift of a child.

Mattie remembered how the tears had fallen as the doctor, with a smile, had given them the news that she was indeed pregnant and in about seven months, give or take a few weeks, would be greeting a new addition to their family.

She had seen the wonder and joy on Ethan's face and knew hers had been a reflection of the same as they held each other and celebrated their good fortune.

Throughout her pregnancy she had been secretly anxious that, because of her age, the baby might be born with problems. Looking down at the perfect little person that she and Ethan had created, she could finally put to rest her fears and breathe a sigh of relief that all was well and as it should be.

Mattie could not resist picking up the sleeping child so she could hold it close to her heart and kiss its tiny head. Her fingers gently stroked the thick, soft dark hair that lay on its head and followed the curve of the tiny eyebrows until she brought them around to caress the downy soft cheeks.

He was perfection!

"Are we still okay with naming him what we decided?" Ethan asked, having woken up to quietly watch her with their son.

"Wyatt for your father, Carter for my maiden name and Goodwin for our family name. Yes, I think it fits him perfectly." Mattie said, sealing the deal with a kiss as Ethan bent over her to taste her lips before bestowing a kiss on Wyatt's head.

A soft tap on the door brought both their heads around as a nurse poked her head in before entering.

"Good morning," she said softly, before coming all the way in and stopping beside the bed. "How are we doing this morning?" she asked, meeting the new parents' eyes with a gentle smile.

"Just fine," Mattie supplied, adjusting the bundle in her arms as Wyatt woke and stirred.

"My name is Hillery," the nurse supplied, as she lifted a clipboard with papers on it and began to write. "I've brought the paperwork to be filled out and thought now would be a good time to get it out of the way before visitors begin arriving."

"That's fine." Ethan agreed, sitting back in the chair he had spent the night in. "What do you need?"

"We just need to get the birth certificate filled out and then I can leave you three alone." Hillery replied, pausing with the pen over the paper.

"What name is this little angel to have?" Hillery asked, as she peered at the baby.

"Let me introduce you to Wyatt Carter Goodwin." Ethan said, with pride in his voice and love in his eyes.

"Wyatt Carter Goodwin," Hillery wrote. "A fine name."

Both Ethan and Mattie smiled in agreement.

Hillery filled in the name of mother and father before looking at her notes and completing her task with the date of birth, time, weight and length. Nodding her head, she tucked the clipboard under her arm and reached out a hand to lay it on the baby's head.

"Welcome to the world." she said. "My wish for you is to have a long and happy life, filled with love and good fortune." she finished. But instead of the soft glow that usually followed her blessings, an icy chill traveled from the baby to her hand and up her arm.

Wyatt opened his eyes and, for just an instant, the bright, baby blue once again turned black as night, as they seemed to glare up in defiance at the Guardian that always blessed the new born humans.

Hillery withdrew her hand and masked her fright as she knew this one was marked by the Dark.

"Well, congratulations," she said, backing up until she reached the door. By the time she did, the child's eyes that followed her had turned back to blue and the facade of innocence was again in place.

Going out the door she placed her completed paperwork on the desk and turned to walk down the long hallway. Her form became dim, but instead of fading away with a feeling of a job well done, she snapped her impressive wings open and took to the air, calling Saul's name as she went.

"Saul!" she cried. "Saul I need you!" and went searching for their leader, hoping it was not too late.

"Was it?" she wondered, "Was it?"

Chapter 5

Saul listened quietly to the words Hillery spoke, never letting on that her news alarmed him in any way. But it did!

He took in everything Hillery had to say before laying a hand upon her shoulder and thanking her for giving him this news. Only then did he step back and allow her to leave.

Saul felt a rush of wind but had no need to turn around as he knew who had come to join him.

"I assume you heard," he said, as Ashton moved to join him.

"I did," was all Ashton said, not giving in to the urge to say "I told you so!" but Saul could detect it in her tone anyway.

Saul's mouth twitched at the corners before he shook his head and let his shoulders slump just a little.

"What do you propose we do?" Saul asked, giving Ashton a chance to voice her opinion.

Ashton walked away from Saul slowly, giving herself time to collect her thoughts before returning and facing him squarely.

"It is my first instinct to end this right now," she said, pausing, waiting for Saul to agree or not. But the Immortal stood silent, forcing Ashton to own her part of the decision.

"But..." she said slowly before pausing once again.

"But what?" Saul asked shortly.

"But maybe we should try and save this soul," Ashton said, swallowing the bad taste in her mouth that the words she had just uttered left behind.

"I think we can try," Saul agreed, relieved and glad that Ashton had come to this decision on her own without him having to argue for it.

"I know this soul was given to me to guide, but if you would be willing to help I would gladly share this task with you," he offered, knowing she would be in the background watching with or without his permission.

Ashton nodded her head in agreement and, smiling at Saul, drew in a deep breath.

"Shall we go see what the damage is?" Ashton asked, opening her wings and prepared to fly.

"I'm right behind you," Saul said, as he bent his knees and gave a powerful lunge.

Two sets of wings sent the wind howling as the Guardians took flight, planning as they made their way, to the human they were going to battle the Dark for.

But they were too late.

It had already begun.

Chapter 6

Saul and Ashton arrived at the Hospital, but instead of the scene they were expecting, that of a family making ready to travel home, they arrived in time to see Ethan sitting on the frozen ground, holding Mattie in his arms as tears rolled down his face.

The day had gone exactly as expected, as tests were conducted and the ok was given for the mother and baby to be released.

Ethan left the room while Mattie got dressed, taking care of the paperwork and bringing the pickup around to the doors where he had been told Mattie and Wyatt would be brought out. He made sure the heater was on full blast and the new car seat in the back was ready for its passenger before getting out and waiting for his family to be brought to him.

He whistled a little as he waited, itching to get home and settle into a new routine. He didn't have to wait long as Mattie, riding in a wheelchair, came into view. He could barely see his wife behind the vase of red roses he had bought her, but he knew she was smiling as widely as he as she held the flowers in her lap.

Two nurses, Ethan, Mattie and Wyatt made their way out to the warm vehicle.

Ethan opened the door and the nurse holding the baby stepped forward placing Wyatt in his new seat, making sure he was properly buckled in before turning with a last good bye and left, leaving the other nurse bending over, intending to hand Ethan the flowers before helping Mattie to stand. Mattie waved her hand away and stood on her own with the beautiful flowers in one arm and reached for Ethan with the other.

Time stopped as Ethan watched the smile leave Mattie's face, along with the rosy color in her cheeks that had been there just an instant before. Her cheeks turned pale and she looked with questioning eyes at him before dropping the vase to the ground at his feet.

No longer was the ground white with the new snow. The vase of beautiful red roses now lay shattered where Mattie had dropped them, contrasting against the sparkling whiteness only for a moment, before the deep red that flowed from Mattie blurred and mixed their color, until all was red.

Ethan's waiting arms caught Mattie as the remaining nurse sped back into the hospital to sound the alarm.

He lowered her onto his lap and held her close, trying to give her comfort and reassure her all would be well, all the while wondering where the hell the hospital staff was. What was taking so long?

He felt the warm wetness that was Mattie's blood soak his legs and he held her tighter, trying to will her to stay with him.

Raising a limp hand, Mattie placed it on her one loves cheek and felt his own tremble as he gripped it and held it in place.

"I love you!" she said, her voice weak but filled with the love she carried in her slowing heart.

"I love you, too" Ethan said, saying the words she needed to hear. "Don't go" he begged softly, his voice shaking as tears slowly fell from his eyes.

"It's okay" Mattie said, tipping her head back from the warmth of his strong neck. "It doesn't hurt."

Ethan didn't want to hear these words and he screamed in his heart for someone, something to help him save his wife. He couldn't see Ashton as she knelt behind Mattie and took her pain into her immortal being.

He couldn't see the fire that burned from the Guardian's body as she raged at the life that was ending too soon.

He never felt Saul lay his hands upon his shivering shoulders as the Guardian helped ease his pain of loss, trying to help him accept.

He never knew that Saul and Ashton gave him a few extra minutes to say and hear the good byes that no one wanted to utter. No one wanted to hear.

All he knew was he never wanted to let Mattie go. Go somewhere he could not follow.

"Tell Wyatt his mother loved him so much" she said, her sight beginning to go dark.

Ethan lowered his lips and kissed the cool lips before he whispered his last "I love you!" to Mattie before he felt her take her last breath. Before she drooped against his chest and left him alone.

The Doctors and nurses came too late to take her from his arms and work to bring life back into her body.

Mattie's spirit stood with Ashton and Saul as she watched her strong husband break with his grief, unable to do anything to stop his pain.

"Come," Saul said, as he took the new spirit's hand. "You must leave this place and begin a new journey."

Mattie watched as a sheet was pulled over her mortal body and the Doctor opened the door to speak with Ethan.

"There is nothing more for you to do here."

"Why?" Mattie asked, as she began to rise with the Guardian.

Ashton never heard Saul's answer as they disappeared but she turned her eyes to the baby that lay in the bed he had been placed on by a nurse.

The infant eyes, that should have been closed in sleep, were open. Ashton's chest filled with rage as she saw the pitch black shining from the innocent face.

She took a step towards the baby, meaning to pull the soul from its tiny body, but stopped as she heard laughter coming from many Dark throats.

She looked into the shadowy corners in this room of death and was forced to bide her time.

Dark Minions huddled together and their leader, Roman, watched her to see what she would do.

"Run away little Guardian!" Roman taunted. "This day belongs to me. This day and this soul are mine."

Ashton ground her teeth in frustration, but she knew to fight so many alone would only end in her death as well.

"I'll be back!" she vowed, as she left to sound a warning. "This is far from over."

Roman hoped she was right as she disappeared, leaving him to gloat over his victory.

The first blow had been dealt by the side of Darkness, but he knew that the Guardians would not give up without a fight.

"Bring it on" He whispered.

"We'll be waiting."

Chapter 7

Saul had escorted Mattie until they stood before the gates which she was to pass through.

"Will I ever see Ethan again?" she asked, her spirit unsettled as she fought her new situation.

Saul smiled with compassion and told her, "When it is time for Ethan to join you, you will indeed be together."

"But how long must I wait?" she asked, not letting it go until she had all of her questions answered.

Saul lifted his head and looked at something Mattie could not see. "It will be many years yet," he said. "Human years that is. To you it will seem hardly more than the blink of an eye."

Mattie calmed as the gates before her opened so she could pass through and be greeted with loving arms by those who had gone before.

"Please take care of him," she said before the gates closed.

"I will," Saul assured her, and lifted his hand in farewell as the gates closed and she was lost from his sight.

Saul stood where she had left him, wondering what lay beyond the massive gates.

Guardians were not allowed to enter, their jobs ending when the departed spirits reached this point. He always hoped it was a place where they would know no pain, no sorrow, no hunger or loneliness. Only happiness and love.

Before he could leave, the skies rumbled and the clouds rolled, letting him know that he was about to be joined by another Immortal Guardian.

"You have news?" he asked, knowing it was Ashton who landed beside him.

"It was the Dark!" she said, without mincing words. "They showed themselves. The baby has been marked as one of theirs and it was Roman himself who told me."

Saul knew a deep anger as he, once again, must lay the blame for a human's death at Leonard's feet. But this time Leonard had the help of the Dark when he caused pain and death.

"What are we going to do?" Ashton asked, willing to follow Saul's lead.

"Fight!" Saul ground out. "We are going to watch and thwart every attempt to completely turn this soul to the Dark side."

"I will fight," Ashton said, standing straight and tall. "I will watch over Wyatt and make sure he is not allowed to kill another living soul."

"Very well," Saul conceded. "I will leave this to you. But should you need help you only have to call and I will come. You will not be alone."

"Thank you Saul," Ashton said, as she grasped his hand in unity. Together they leapt into the air and disappeared from sight.

In their place Sam now stood as he clenched his fists in rage. He had heard all and he knew that Ashton would be putting herself in danger to protect the little turd that had once again derailed another destiny with his Dark ways.

"No she won't be alone!" he thought, as he snapped out his wings preparing to follow her.

"Jaxon! Hunter!" he called, as his wings heaved with power.

Both of the Guardians came when called and, as they flew through the clouds, Sam filled them in on what had happened and why.

Ashton and Saul may have made their plans but the three Immortals that now joined the fray were making their own.

And they would not be so nice!

Chapter 8

Ethan opened his eyes to the grey light of a new day. The pain of Mattie's passing did not give him a moment's peace, raising its ugly head to dig at his insides until he groaned with its weight.

It had been a month since he had laid Mattie in the ground and made the attempt to get on with his life. If it had not been for their son he might just have laid down and died himself, so empty was his life without her. But he couldn't.

Every morning he pulled himself out of bed and, for the first few seconds, dealt with the loss of his wife, wondering when the pain would dull. Everyone said it would, but so far they had all got it wrong. The pain was still a knife in his heart and a burning in his belly. His soul rumbled with the loss of its mate and he felt broken anew as he opened his tired eyes once again to start a new day.

Sam had stood by Ethan's bed every morning since Mattie's death and helped the mortal man deal with his heartache. He knew, first hand, what it was like to lose the one you loved. Every morning as he pulled Ethan's pain into his being, he remembered his own agonizing pain when Ashton had been taken from him. But this was a small price to pay for Sam to insure that this father could muster the strength and will to get up and make a life for his new son, Mattie's and his son.

Once a week Sam left one small feather on Ethan's pillow as a sign that his Guardian's were watching over him. And every day, when Ethan found the feather, Sam smiled as the human grumbled and wondered when he was going to have to replace his pillow, thinking the feathers had escaped during the night. But Sam did not give up the ritual. Even though Ethan did not understand the significance of this gesture, Sam did and that was good enough for him.

While Sam attended to the father, Ashton looked in on Wyatt. Every morning she placed her immortal hands, hands that burned with a cleansing fire, on the small body and pulled the darkness that had grown in him out until she was able to turn it to ash and leave the boy as clean as she could make him.

Try as she might, she could never reach the seed that Roman had planted in the tiny soul. So every day she did what she could to allow goodness to grow, hoping maybe one day it would be strong enough to kill the darkness that remained. But today was not that day.

Ashton was dusting off her hands when she was joined by Guardians Jaxon and Hunter after checking the property for Dark Minions.

Ashton crossed her arms over her chest and waited for the two to tell her why each wore a satisfied grin on their faces.

"We found a couple of Roman's lackeys hanging around so we had a bit of fun with them." Jaxon supplied for both, sharing a smile of secrets held back with Hunter.

Ashton did not ask for details, having seen first hand what both did to the Dark Ones that they caught causing mischief and chaos.

Her own hands had burned many to ash but she did not play with them as Jaxon and Hunter were apt to do. She was only surprised that she had not heard the dying screams as they died a slow and painful death, their black blood sending a message to Roman that if he was smart he would cut his losses and run from these protected humans.

But no one ever accused Roman of being smart when it came to souls he wanted.

The smile of victory left Jaxon's face as he watched Ethan enter the room. He could see the bone deep sadness in the depths of this mortals eyes and he balled his fists in anger that he could do nothing to ease his pain.

A growl rumbled in his chest and Jaxon bent his knees ready to leap as the urge to hunt the Dark offenders grew in him.

"Why don't we take off?" Hunter suggested, giving Jaxon's shoulder a hard squeeze. "I think Sam and Ashton can handle things from here."

"Yes, why don't we?" Jaxon answered, and the light that flared in his dark eyes was cold and promised death to those he hunted.

"Call if you need us." Hunter said, before nodding farewell to Ashton and leapt into the air.

"You know I'm glad those two are on our side." Sam said, as he came up behind Ashton and gathered her into his strong arms.

"Me too," Ashton agreed, as she leaned into her soul mates body.

Both were quiet as they watched Ethan lean over the crib and gather Wyatt up in gentle arms, and both knew jealousy as he snuggled the warm bundle to his chest before leaving the room to change the diaper and dress his little one in clean warm clothes for the day.

"I think our work here is done for now." Sam said, giving Ashton a squeeze and a kiss before grabbing her hand and preparing to depart.

"Be safe," Ashton said, speaking to the small Guardian kitten that rode upon the back of the protective family pet. "Call if you have troubles."

"I will," Callie purred. "Don't worry."

Ashton reached out a hand and stroked the soft fur before taking her leave.

Callie was small but her soul was that of a lion, and when the need arose she came out with teeth bared, claws unfurled and with a roar that shook the ground.

The Goodwin's were safe.

For today.

Chapter 9

Ethan found a small measure of peace in the morning ritual he and Wyatt had developed. Getting up, getting dressed, getting fed, and when the burping and pooping were done it was time for the outside chores. Not that there were many.

Ethan's neighbors were kind and decent folks lending a hand with what needed to be done around the ranch. "That's what friends do," they told him. That's what friends were for. He would do the same for them, and he would have even though he hoped with all his heart none of them would have the same reason for needing his help as he did theirs.

The men came in their trucks helping to feed the cattle, and even staying to make sure each calf that was born hit the ground running. Not one had been lost this year, and Ethan was grateful for each pair of hands that did what he was not able to do.

He did what he could outside, but he kept the biggest share of Wyatt's care for himself. Needing to hold a piece of Mattie in his arms, giving his love to their child.

The wives and daughters of his neighbors came and insisted on cleaning the house, doing the dishes and laundry and making food for the day so he would not have to cook. They knew he wouldn't have if left on his own.

At first Ethan had left his son in the care of the women when he went outside to check on his livestock, but it had only taken three weeks before he came up with the idea to take him along.

Jumping in his pickup one morning after the chores were done and Wyatt was down for a nap, Ethan drove to town. He was on a mission.

Stopping at the local super center, he walked with purpose through the sliding doors and headed straight to the baby section. He knew the way by heart now, having made numerous trips to pick up diapers, formula, wipes and the trillion other things that no baby could live without.

He walked the isles until he found what he was looking for, one of those strap on harness things that you carried the baby around on your chest with. He stripped off his coat and tried one after another on until he found one that was built like a tow rope and fit his chest with ease.

Next he hit the men's clothing section and found a huge coat that would cover not only him but the new contraption and his son as well.

By the time this was done Ethan was sweating like a pig from making his many decisions and trying on half the clothes in the store. Walking out, he decided he had definitely been born without the shopping gene but he had sucked it up and felt pleased as he drove home with his wares.

The men nodded their heads in understanding and took turns pulling on the heavy duty straps until all were satisfied that the strange thing would not break, probably lasting until the boy hit his teenage years and then some.

The women were another story. When he explained his plan to them they let out shrieks of horror at the idea that Ethan wanted to take this poor baby out in the cold. Well they had never heard of such a thing and talked until they were blue in the face trying to make him see reason. But Ethan stood his ground and let them talk. After they threw out all their objections, he thanked them and still did exactly as he wanted.

So every morning he got himself up and did what he needed to do around the house until Wyatt woke. Usually by then someone was there to help him feed and cloth his son.

With full bellies and dry pants Ethan would pick up Wyatt, telling him it was time for them to do the mans work outside. He then proceeded to kiss him and strap him to his chest, covering them both with the big coat and headed for the door, extra bottle and diaper in his pocket. Better safe than sorry, he figured, as he took his boy out to greet the new day.

After about a week the female population finally calmed down, seeing that the baby was well cared for and did not get sick or die as they were all sure he would.

They also saw the way it made Ethan feel, happy and content to have someone to share his day with. It was a piece of Mattie he carried with him. None were aware of the feelings of loss and loneliness he woke with every day. The pain he carried in his heart and the open wound that not even Sam and Ashton were able to completely heal were his constant companions. But he lived. He had to. For Wyatt. Every day. He lived.

And so the days went. Ethan and Wyatt spending almost every waking minute together until the weather calmed and father and son put away the heavy coat, exchanging it for a light sweat shirt that was not so warm but still gave protection to the growing child.

The front carrier gave way to a back one that allowed Ethan to still have his son with him, while allowing his hands to be more able to do the chores that came with the spring thaw.

When it came time to ready the cows and their calves to be put out to pasture, Ethan was forced to leave his companion with a sitter. He did not want to take the chance of one or both of them getting injured if an over protective mother decided to investigate why her baby was crying and give chase until the offender was high up a fence, out of her reach.

When the livestock was tended to and all that could be done was finished, one by one the men left to tend to their own herds, until it was just Ethan and Wyatt at home.

He had offered to help in return for all his friends had done, but with a slap on the back and a handshake all refused but assured him if the need arose they would call on him.

Ethan watched the dust fade as the last pick up drove away and he was left alone with the active bundle gurgling on his back and a silent home to greet them as they called it a day.

A bump to his hip brought Ethan back to the present and he looked down to find Gabriel standing next to him, tongue out and eyes bright with his love for his human.

"Let's go inside buddy," Ethan said, stroking the massive warm head. "We made it through another day. Let's go home."

Together the three made their way across the lawn that was just now starting to green up, until they entered their home and closed the door on the setting sun.

Spring was a time for new beginnings, but Ethan just saw the end of each day as one more day he had been able to get through without Mattie.

"Would he ever get over this?" he wondered as he lay his head down on his pillow.

Callie landed on the bed and lay by the mortal's head, purring in his ear until he fell asleep, her sweet song of comfort bringing him peace. Only dreams of happiness to keep him company through the night were allowed, but even she could not stop the bitter tear of loneliness that crept out of his closed eye and wet his pillow.

The Immortal feline mewed in sadness and wished she could give him what it would take to make him whole again.

But she could not, no one could.

Sometimes life was unfair.

Chapter 10

Ethan pulled his pickup to a stop in front of his door and shut off the engine. Taking the baseball cap from his head he swiped at the sweat on his forehead before replacing it and slumping back against the seat. Feeling hot and tired had nothing to do with the warmer temperatures or even from over exertion. Nope, none of the above.

Father and son had just returned from a trip into town. Glancing into the rear view mirror, Ethan had the strong urge to join his son in an afternoon nap to recover from the dreaded ordeal.

After a moment of peace and quiet, with only the shrill calls of the birds as music, he gave a sigh of resignation, and telling himself that the worst was behind him, he opened his door and made ready to lift his son out of his car seat. He took him inside before returning to heft out the sacks of groceries that would stock his shelves for the near future.

Only the lonely sound of a clock ticking greeted Ethan as he opened the door to lay his son down in a playpen set up in the living room so he could have him close at hand when he awoke.

A small frown marred his brow as Ethan looked down at the tiny chest rising and falling with each innocent breath.

Visions of their time in town popped into his head and he put his hands deep into his pockets as he mulled each one over at length.

When Ethan hit the edge of town he could've sworn that some secret women's radar went off, letting all the single females know that available prey had entered their territory and the hunt was afoot.

No matter where he went he was tracked down by these amazons and hung on, clung to and squeezed, until he wanted to shake himself like a wet dog to get them off him. Being the gentleman that he was he gave each his attention and was polite to every single, and single being the operative word, one of them. Not so his son.

Wyatt sat in his stroller and watched with quiet eyes as the females flocked to his father and gushed over his every word. After the first initial greeting they would bend down and stick their faces close to his and try to get him to smile at them as they grabbed his hand or pinched his cheek. He was having none of that and Ethan had to apologize over and over for his reaction as they pulled back with scratched hands or red faces where his tiny hands had connected in rejection.

More than once Ethan had wondered if he could find a sign that read, instead of beware of dog, beware of child. That way they approached at their own risk and he could say they had been forewarned of any injury they may come away with.

Ethan stood pondering his son's behavior until the change in his pockets tinkled like wind chimes in a harsh wind. But he came no closer to an answer as to why his son seemed to hate the women. He didn't seem to object to the men as much, but maybe that was because most of their visitors now-days were his neighbors and friends, and most stopped by without their wives in tow.

"I wish you were here Mattie," he thought for the thousandth time, feeling her influence would have made all the difference in the world when it came to their son's anti-social behavior and bad manners.

Callie mewed softly into Gabriel's ear, letting him know that his master needed a friend until the dog nudged his human, letting him know that he was there and always would be.

Ethan came back to the present and, pulling a hand out of his pocket, reached down to stroke the soft, warm fur on his buddy's head.

"I still got you, don't I boy?" he asked, as he knelt down and wrapped his arms around the strong neck.

Gabriel leaned into those arms and huffed out a happy sigh, needing nothing more than to be close and feel loved by this man. He licked the face close to his and gave a soft whine of pleasure until Ethan pulled back.

Giving him one last squeeze and looking him straight in the eyes, Ethan planted a kiss on the massive head.

"I love you too, buddy." he said, his heart glad that this dog was his.

Callie purred in approval at the bond these two shared and enjoyed a stretch before curling into a ball on the wide shoulders of her charge. She would stay there and watch over them both as Ashton had instructed her to. Nothing would sneak up on them while she was on guard

Her Immortal eyes tracked over until they rested on the sleeping boy before becoming still and alert.

This one was bad. She knew it before Ashton had told her. She could smell it. So she watched, not only for the Dark that lived in the shadows, but for the Dark that lived in this mortal's soul.

She knew the reason Wyatt lashed out at the women that tried to win his approval, and it concerned her much.

Even though Ashton came every morning to pull the Darkness from the small soul, it began to grow as soon as she left. And it was growing faster each day.

Callie knew, as did Ashton, that this could not continue. But until the day came that the Darkness took over and a war must be fought, she would watch and protect as best she could.

A soft growl rumbled her chest and her claws grew long with the thought of a battle to come.

"But not today," she calmed herself.

"Not today." she thought, as she relaxed her body but not her mind.

Just not today.

But soon!

Chapter 11

It seemed to take nothing more than a blink of an eye for time to pass, and before Ethan knew what was happening, he was walking Wyatt into school for his first day of kindergarten.

Looking down at the small child at his side he almost didn't recognize him as the son who he had raised on his own.

The fresh hair cut and the shiny clean face were not what he was used to seeing everyday. His memories were more of hair that was constantly mussed from the wind and a face that had dirt rings around a mouth that constantly asked *why* and *how come*?

Clean clothes in the mornings gave way to dirt and grass stains from playing with his tractors and their attachments, as he tried to mimic the actions of the man he looked up to.

Ethan felt his heart tear as the hand he held in his pulled away, seeming to have no qualms about being left on his own with strangers.

Not knowing what to do with his now empty hand, Ethan stuck it deep in his pocket and shuffled his feet, wondering if he should go or what the normal procedure was exactly. Looking around at the other parents, he could tell who the first timers, like himself, were and which ones had already been there and done that.

Ones like himself stood where they had been left, looking lost and on the verge of tears. While the old pros looked more like they were happy to finally have a free day to themselves, flapping their hands in good-bye as they headed out the door.

Catching the watchful eye of the teacher, Ethan cocked his head in question and pointed at the door asking permission to take his leave. A soft smile and a nod from the teacher let him know his part in Wyatt's first day was at an end.

The hall, in comparison to the noise of twenty small voices, was quiet and his boots echoed with each step he took, making him want to tip-toe until he got outside.

When he finally did reach his pickup and climbed inside, his hands trembled as they reached for the keys. He was half-way home before his heart stopped pounding in his chest and the urge to turn around and snatch his son back up had passed. 'Who would have known that leaving his son at school would be so traumatic?' he wondered.

Ethan kept himself busy during the day doing what needed to be done. But that didn't stop him from checking his watch every hour, and thinking the day seemed a hundred years long.

As four o'clock neared, Ethan stopped working and strolled to the end of his driveway, fixing his eyes on the road, not wanting to miss the bus as it pulled up for the first time. 'There were a lot of firsts today," he mused, leaning against the mailbox that had Goodwin printed on it.

Five minutes later he straightened, as a cloud of dust began to grow in the distance. Not long after that, the same dust settled as the bus came to a noisy stop right in front of him. The door opened and a smile grew on his face as his son bounced down the steps and ran to his side.

"Hey buddy," Ethan said, a broad smile on his face. "How was it?"

He found he did not have to do more than nod his head as Wyatt sang the praises of his first day at school.

What he didn't tell his father though was the fact he had been made to sit in the corner in a time out for fighting with another boy.

The fact that Brady Collins was two inches taller than Wyatt had no effect on the outcome when he asked in a snide voice, "Where's your mother? I heard you killed her when you were born."

Happy blue eyes turned cold and black as the dark seed planted in the human soul growled with glee at its first chance of freedom. It whispered encouragement of retaliation, and the small fist that flew in revenge connected with the bully's nose, leaving blood flowing and the first taste of darkness sweet on Wyatt's tongue.

Wyatt didn't tell his father that he had made his first enemy and that he looked forward to anything this Brady wanted to dish out.

He didn't tell his father how he had felt strong and powerful when his fist had connected with flesh and he had been the one to cause another pain.

He didn't tell his father how the voice in his head had cheered him on and praised him for doing what had to be done.

He didn't tell his father the secret he now harbored in his heart, that it had felt good to attack another.

No, he didn't tell!

Chapter 12

Ashton stood beside the bed of the one she still knew as Leonard. It was hard for her to think of him as anything else. She had been doing this since Saul had placed Leonard's soul into this human form. But every day, since this boy had gotten out into the world, it became more of a challenge to rid him of the darkness that clung to him like a disease.

Every morning, before he woke, she placed her hands on him and fought to pull the darkness out that grew bigger and stronger each day. Hands that burned with fire dug deep, but never deep enough, as the seed that Roman had planted hung on with talons of steel, refusing to give up its host.

Roman wanted this one and he meant to have him, no matter the cost. And the cost to Ethan was high.

The grey that colored Ethan's temples and streaked his dark hair was mostly because of the son that had gone from a sweet little boy to a rebellious teenager without him being aware that something was terribly wrong.

Small things, like keepsakes being broken, flowers being pulled up, rips and tears appearing in clothes and furniture, and dishes being broken were all put down to accidents and/or normal everyday mistakes. But when Ethan looked back on everything he began to wonder if it was indeed mishaps or was it something more. He just didn't want to see it.

Trouble at school was becoming more and more frequent, with his son being the cause of fights, vandalism, and the instigator of discord. Or so they told Ethan on his many visits to the principal's office.

Wyatt had been there so many times he was sure the seat had his butt print permanently imprinted on it.

For the umpteenth time Ethan hung up the phone after agreeing to appear at the school and have another talk with the principal about an incident that had occurred today. His shoulders slumped and his hair stood on end from having agitated fingers run through it, over and over again.

"What to do?" he wondered. "What to do?"

As Ethan sat at the kitchen table trying to make sense of his son, Sam quietly appeared at his side. Sam wished he could fix the problems that plagued this mortal, but all he could do was once again lay his comforting hands upon Ethan's shoulders and drink in the feelings of failure that coursed through his body and tore at his mind.

"It's not your fault," Sam said, as he bent down and whispered in this father's ear. "You are doing all you can."

"Am I?" Ethan said out loud, thinking he was talking to himself. "Maybe if I had found a good woman and remarried Wyatt would have had a more normal life and things would be different now."

"Could've, would've, should've have no place here," Sam lectured. "You are a fine father and the fault should not rest on your shoulders."

"Really?" Ethan scoffed. "I'm the adult here and it is up to me to set a good example for my son to follow. It should be up to me to teach him to be a good human being."

"You can only do so much before Wyatt must be held accountable for his own actions," Sam advised, gently but firmly.

Heaving one last sigh, Ethan hoisted himself to his feet and grabbed his hat on the way out the door.

"Please let this be the last time," he whispered, closing the door behind him.

Gabriel came to his side and nudged him until a hand was lowered and his soft head gave a small measure of comfort to his friend.

Ethan wanted to bury his face in the massive neck and rest in the warmth offered to him but he didn't want to be late.

"I'll be back soon," he said to the faithful dog. "Keep our home safe until we get back." and with a final stroke to the head, he made his way down the steps and into his waiting vehicle.

Gabriel and Callie watched as he drove out of sight. A soft whine broke from the dog as he lay down and put his head on his paws. Callie used her small paws to kneed the thick neck and ease the tension and sadness that Gabriel had picked up from Ethan

"Be on guard," she purred into the canine ear. "I smell trouble." She felt the body under her tense and the eyes that had been clouded with sadness cleared and became watchful.

"You shall not pass!" Gabriel growled out. "No one or no thing shall do harm to my family. Stay away!" he growled low in his throat. "Stay away or deal with me!"

From the afternoon shadows a wet laugh taunted. Roman was not impressed. 'It would take more than a mortal dog to keep him at bay,' he smirked. 'Much more!'

Callie arched her back and gave a hiss of warning that carried up until it reached Ashton, Sam, Jaxon and Hunter. She was alerting the Cavalry and hoped their numbers would chase away the leader of the Dark before he could cause mischief, or worse.

Gabriel too sensed the Dark and his body tensed until he was as tight as a drum. His lips curled back from his sharp teeth and drool fell from his mouth as his growl rumbled way down deep in his chest.

The air whipped as Ashton, Sam, Jaxon, Hannah, Hunter and Dee all came to rest behind Callie and her charge.

Roman backed farther into the shadows and taunted from a safe distance. "Well, well, well. It looks like the gang's all here!" he needled. "Except for your fearless leader that is. Too scared to face me, is he?"

Jaxon crossed one foot over the other as he leaned with nonchalance against Hannah. The smile that bloomed on his face was not one given to a friend, but held ice under the thin veneer of civility.

"Anxious to die are we?" he questioned, distracting the Dark Leader.

The shadows around Roman deepened with his anger and he made to step forward, intending to kill at least one on this day. But one word from behind him made him rethink his actions. Rethink them and flee in fright.

"Boo!"

Roman screamed.

Saul laughed.

Chapter 13

Saul dusted off his hands in a gesture that conveyed a job well done before joining his friends to see why they were all called here.

"I assume we were called because of Roman." he stated, looking to Callie for confirmation.

"Yes" Callie mewed, as she jumped from her perch on Gabriel's shoulders to the waiting arms of Dee. "It concerned me that the Leader of the Dark made an appearance. So I thought it would be wise to have back-up in case he decided to cause harm to my charge," she said, glancing to the massive dog that cocked his head as if listening.

Saul moved to the side of the beast and stroked the soft fur with immortal hands, letting him know that he was a valued part of their team as a protector.

"Yes, you were wise to call," Saul agreed, and turned his attention back to the Guardians who stood before him.

“It’s getting harder to protect this human and his father, you know,” Jaxon said, standing up straight and tall, giving Saul the respect he had denied Roman.

“What makes this soul so special to Roman?” Jaxon asked. He wanted to know, feeling they were all due an explanation.

Saul looked at the Guardians standing before him, all waiting to hear why they were fighting unusually hard for this soul. Why Roman had such a hard-on for this one ordinary human.

“I can only guess as to his reasoning, but I will tell you what I think,” Saul began.

“When Leonard was one of us I think Roman had hopes of turning him and planting him among us to turn other Guardians to his Dark cause.”

Saul paused and looked directly at Jaxon, making the fierce Immortal hunter arch a dark brow and curl his lip in anger.

“Don’t look at me!” Jaxon growled “I made my choice on the night I died. Remember?”

“But I think Roman would count it as a major victory if he or one of his followers could get you to flip to his side,” Saul said, with a shrug of his broad shoulders.

“Dream on!” Jaxon growled low in his throat, his muscles turning to rocks as he allowed his hatred for the Dark to show. “Those Dark bastards don’t have a snowball’s chance in hell of turning me!” he spat.

“Be calm my friend.” Saul said, resting a comforting hand on his hunter’s shoulder. “I have never doubted you fight for the side of good, and always will.”

"Then what are we going to do?" Hunter wanted to know, jumping into the conversation.

"We do what we have been doing all along," Saul said. "We keep the Dark from getting their claws into Wyatt as best we can."

"For how long?" Ashton wanted to know. "It gets harder and harder to pull the blackness from Wyatt everyday. I fear before long I will not be able to burn enough out of him to make a difference. Then what?"

Saul's eyes became sad and his shoulders seemed to bow under the weight of knowing the day would come when the choice of action would be taken from him. He and his Immortal friends who fought at his side to keep the Dark from ruling the Earth.

"When that happens," Saul replied, his voice becoming stronger with each word he spoke. "When the day comes that we can no longer protect the humans from this soul's Dark plan, we fight!"

"We fight until we can fight no more! We keep on fighting until the battle field runs deep with the foul blood of our enemy. And when we are too tired to fight, we fight some more!"

As Saul spoke the ground shook and the air burned with the feelings he unleashed.

Blinding white wings that were hidden on his back opened until they framed the mighty Immortal, opened until the power Saul projected made them shine brighter that the hottest star.

The Dark vultures, that spied from the shadows, shrieked as the shadows they hid in disappeared and their dying screams told all who heard of the power of light unleashed.

Saul's power burned until it was reflected back at him in the eyes of the Immortal warriors that fought at his side.

Wings were snapped open and, as one, their voices roared out a challenge to the Dark that all who picked up the gauntlet of war would have to fight to the death! Nothing else would be accepted!

Death was on the menu and death was what would be served!

But whose was yet to be seen.

Saul's heart broke as he looked upon the Guardians that had become his friends, his family. Who would be sacrificed for the cause that would take so much from him before the fight was over?

Who would this war against evil claim before they could call victory?

"Not my friends!" he prayed. *"Please, just this once, not my friends!"*

Time would tell.

Chapter 14

Roman gnashed his blackened, broken teeth as he paced his dark dungeon in frustration.

He had let his guard down for only an instant. So intent was he on wiping the insolent smirk off Jaxon's face, that Saul had been able to surprise him from behind. A rookie mistake on his part and one that could have cost him dearly if Saul had wanted to strike.

He would almost have preferred the strike instead of the slap he received to his ego with the stupid "boo" his rival had uttered.

"Stupid! Stupid! Stupid!" Roman muttered, wanting to take out his anger on someone, but there was no one to blame but himself.

Not one of his minions dared to enter Roman's chambers when he was in a mood, having learned many times over that to do so would be suicide. They skulked in the dark until called. Until the oozing voice of their master summoned one of them to his side.

And they did not have long to wait, as Roman came up with a plan to further his cause.

Settling himself in the dark, Roman sent out his summons to the one he wanted before him.

"Haven." he commanded. "Haven, come to me!"

The dark spirit he called was not one of the ones hiding outside his chambers. This Haven could have cared less about her Master's bad mood or the reason for it. She had her own trouble to cause and went about it with Dark intent.

Receiving a call from Roman only served to irritate her and make her mutter under her breath as she peeled off from what she was doing to obey the command.

Roman waited until the dark, smoky figure appeared before him to relax and seat himself upon his throne of power.

"What may I do for you Master?" Haven asked, keeping her black eyes lowered in false respect. "How may I serve you?"

Roman was not fooled. He knew that this Dark Spirit held no liking for him and he really could not have given a rat's ass one way or the other. As long as she served a purpose and did not openly defy him he would use her any way he wanted.

"I have a job for you," he informed her, not asking her permission.

"What might that be?" Haven asked, her voice husky and wet.

"There is a mortal I want you to help turn to do my bidding," he said. "A seed of Darkness has already been planted, so all you must do is to help it grow and make sure the Guardians do not catch wind of your intentions."

"Why doesn't the one who sowed the seed finish the job?" she asked, hating to be called on to finish something someone else had started. Why was it that she always got called to clean up a mess some incompetent had screwed up?

"That would be me," Roman said, and was not disappointed in the reaction of his minion as she sucked in air in surprise at his bold statement.

"I planted this seed at birth, and now it is time for it to take root and grow," he supplied, wondering what other questions this unruly one would think up. He could almost see smoke coming from her brain as she tried to come up with a reason for his need of her.

"I'm sending you back in human form to get to know this mortal and do whatever it takes to get him to commit to our way of thinking," he concluded.

Haven bowed her dark head in submission, but she was not stupid. She knew that there had to be a pretty good reason for Roman to pass off an assignment that he had started so easily. And if she was correct, it was going to have to do with the Guardians.

She would have bet his life, not her own, that the Guardians were going to be all over this mortal and she was going to be lucky to get out with her butt still intact.

But she shrugged, her black holes for eyes beginning to glow. It might be just enough of a challenge that she would be able to alleviate the boredom that had plagued her of late.

Always the same crap! Stir up some trouble, turn a few lower level souls, skulk in the shadows. Boring!!!

She wanted something that she could sink her teeth into. Sink them in deep and fill the hunger in her belly for darkness and death.

"Come closer," Roman beckoned with his dirty excuse for a finger. "Let me fill you in on the details, and make no mistake," he threatened, "should you fail in this task it will be the last thing you ever do."

Haven bowed her head, but only to hide her expression of distain.

"I do not fail," she reminded the puffed-up wisp of smoke before her.

"Now tell me what you want done and let me be on my way!" she ground out.

Roman did.

Haven left.

Smiling.

Chapter 15

Wyatt sat in the hall outside the principal's office waiting for his father to show up. *"He's going to be pissed!"* the teen thought to himself. Giving a mental shrug, Wyatt Goodwin slouched lower in the "chair of shame" he had been made to sit in more times than he could count.

It had not taken him long to figure out school sucked, and the only way he could bring himself to attend every day was to think up ways to entertain himself.

The lessons he had to learn each day came far too easy for him to fall into and conform to the norm of the pack of morons that attended his school. Most of them had been in the same school, the same small town and the same rut since kindergarten and, now that it was their senior year, he was so over hearing how they could not wait to graduate and jump right back into the same crap by attending some esteemed college of choice.

The one thing Wyatt would miss would be the sports he actually enjoyed. Like studying, he seemed to have a knack for anything involving physical contact.

Maybe it was because he was allowed to cause pain and the fools actually cheered him for it.

Being a jock allowed him some perks and the teachers and staff often looked the other way when he was caught causing trouble. 'Often' being the operative word here.

Sometimes, like today, they had no choice and he was sent to the office and had to wait for his father to show up. Then he had to sit and promise to be good and not do whatever had gotten him into hot water again. Not too hard of a promise. He just came up with something new the next time. No promises ever broken. Cool.

Wyatt shifted his position in the chair and sat up a little straighter when he spied his father striding down the long hallway.

"Again, Wyatt?" his father asked, barely stopping to acknowledge his handful of a son.

"Sorry, Dad," Wyatt mumbled, not meaning a word of it, before Ethan opened the door and disappeared into the dreaded principal's office.

Just a few short seconds had passed before the door opened again. Wyatt lifted a brow thinking "Wow, that didn't take long." But it wasn't Ethan that came strolling out but a smoking hot girl that Wyatt had never seen before. He would have remembered.

He looked at her, up and down he looked at her, unable to help himself.

What he saw, and coveted, was a short, maybe five foot four inch tall girl with buckets full of long black hair hanging down her back in fat, lush waves. A short, dark skirt hugged a tight, little butt and nicely curved legs ending in some kind of black boot was all he could make out from the back as she walked away from him.

His breath caught in his throat and his heart pounded in his chest until his mouth went dry and his toes actually curled in his expensive tennis shoes when she stopped a few feet from him, turning slowly to face him.

For the first time in his short life Wyatt was speechless and in awe of someone other than himself.

Again Wyatt's eyes traveled from the black boots, up the trim legs, past the little skirt, taking in the grey tee shirt that had luscious bumps that he was sure would fit perfectly in his hands, until his eyes stopped on her face.

He did not dwell on the dark eyes staring at him until he had had his fill of the blood red unsmiling mouth, peaches and cream flawless skin, winged eyebrows and the straight nose with its flared nostrils. He even noticed the small black diamond stud that pierced her nose, before meeting those dark eyes once again. This time falling into their trap until he willingly lay down to die in them.

As he locked his gaze to hers, he felt something stir in his belly. Something dark and strong raised its sleeping head and took notice.

Here was an equal, a partner, a feeder of the Dark.

And it was hungry!

Chapter 16

Haven Strange pulled her sleek black Mustang into a parking place and gave it one more punch of gas before turning the key to off. It was almost a shame to silence the deep growl of power her black beauty purred out.

Since joining the Dark there had only been a couple of times that she had been allowed back in human form, and each time she conjured the only thing she missed from her mortal life. Her car!

When she had been alive she had begged, borrowed and stole whatever she needed to insure that the one thing that brought her pleasure was taken care of.

It may have sounded stupid to some, but her car never lied to her, cheated on her, beat her or tore her down like the people in her life had. In return, she had poured all the love she had in her into it. Ironically it was the reason she died at the early age of seventeen.

Thugs had tried to take the car from her and she had fought back, pulling a knife out, meaning to slice and dice a few chunks out of them before they turned and ran. But you know the old saying, never bring a knife to a gun fight. Haven learned first hand what happened when you did.

She remembered standing over her dead body and staring in shock at the holes that had been put in her, watching the thugs laugh and climb into her car before driving away.

Two beings had come to her, one of light with feathered wings, the other black and twisted with eyes of fire and smoke for breath.

The being of light offered her peace and a chance to fight on the side of good, while the Dark one laughed behind its back until it was time for him to make his offer.

Instead of wings and goodness, it offered darkness and a chance for retribution for her death. She didn't give it a second thought, as she took the Dark hand and never looked back.

She had been taken before Roman where he immediately recognized the anger in her and knew he could use that anger to swell his ranks.

Walking around her, he had made a decision to give her the power of despair. After training her on how to use it, he'd cut her loose to plague the youth of humanity.

But before she could embrace her new existence, she had debts owed to her that she hungered to collect. And she collected them in spades!

She had hunted down the three that had taken her prized possession and her life, taking her sweet time driving them to madness until she allowed them to take their own lives. Not the easy way out, with pills or such, but with pain and horror being their last memories.

One clawed his own eyes out with his bare hands because of the monsters she let him see, asleep and awake. She made sure they were more than any mortal mind could bear. Revenge was indeed sweet!

One down!

The second ended up taking a knife to himself until he had no skin left, as he tried to release the things that crawled beneath it. Things that gnawed at him and caused him such pain, that he would have done anything to end his torment. Peeling his skin off with a razor sharp knife, one inch at a time seemed just the thing to rid him of his torment.

Two down!

The third one, the one that had ended her life with hot lead and no remorse, she saved until last. He had made a powerful enemy and she let that power loose until it rained death down upon him, drowning him in a river of blood that only he could see.

She let him choke on it until he stood before her and begged for mercy.

She gave none, letting the Dark take him to hell and an eternity of suffering as payment for the wrong done to her.

Only then did she take up the Dark cause and add to the number of Roman's army with souls so full of despair they committed the sin of suicide, giving them no choice but to join her in darkness.

Her power of despair was easy to plant in the youth of today, as most of them sat around and whined about how unfair life was and how they were owed everything and wanted what they had not earned. How everything offended them, not because it did, but because it got them noticed and made them feel important. Losers!!

Haven was sure that if she were still alive she would mind her own business and could never see herself acting like the tools that call themselves young adults in this time. But everything played right into her hands as she let them feel the weight of dreams that were unrealistic and envy of what they refused to go out and earn.

Yup, easy pickings!

While others from the Dark side fought to gather souls, her targets almost chased her down, begging for her to claim them as hers.

Haven gathered her thoughts and prepared to lock up her car for the day. Going back to school was not her idea of a great time.

"*This pet project of Romans better be worth it!*" she thought. If not, she was going to make this mortal's life a living hell.

Hmmmm.

The shrill sound of the beginning bell had students pouring through the school's open doors from all directions and Haven decided she might as well join them.

It was time.

It was time to hunt

Chapter 17

Wyatt slowly pushed himself to his feet, straightening until his six feet three inch frame towered over the new girl in school.

Just as he had looked her over, Haven now took her time doing the same and she liked what she saw.

Dark hair, longer than what was popular today, crowned his head and provided a perfect frame for a face that was sinfully gorgeous.

Big sky blue eyes, framed with thick black lashes and winged dark brows, watched her with hunger as she looked her fill. His mouth gave her pause as she imagined pressing her own to it and drinking her fill of him until he panted in passion and begged for more.

It had been a long time since a mortal had stirred Haven the way this one was doing. But she opened herself to the sensations and, as she imagined herself wrapped around the tall, toned young body before her, she planted those same images in his mind, letting him see just what she wanted to do with him, to him.

The jeans he wore, not hanging off his ass by the way, hugged his legs and hips, leaving little to the imagination as he responded to the images she was flooding his mind with.

Haven smiled.

Wyatt wanted.

Tired of standing still, Wyatt took a step forward and, thinking it stupid to hold out his hand for a shake, he stuffed them deep into his pockets to keep from grabbing her to him.

"I'm Wyatt," he said, his voice deep and dry.

"Haven," she responded, having no qualms about reaching her hand out and laying it over his heart.

"*Awwww there it is,*" Haven thought with a sigh, as she felt the squirming of the Dark under his skin, under her hand.

The Dark seed, that had been thwarted everyday, came to life as it recognized one of its kind and ropes of blackness began to creep out to explore the body and mind of the one it lived in.

It crept out slowly, being cautious. It remembered the pain it endured every morning as the foul Guardian, with hands of fire, tried to pull it from this body, making it whimper and retreat. It was careful. It was hopeful. It was ripe and ready to grow and do what it was intended for. It grew bold.

Haven left her hand right where she had placed it until the human, her human, raised his own to cover the black nailed appendage with his much warmer, larger one.

She let the seedling feed off her darkness until it took from her what it needed to spread and become unstoppable.

Wyatt did not usually go for the strange girls that walked the halls dressed in black, looking spooky and kind of creepy, but this one made his blood boil. Something about her called to him and, being the walking hormone that most teenage boys were, he answered that call with relish.

"You're new here," Wyatt said, making conversation to keep her from walking away.

"Duh, captain obvious," Haven thought, rolling her eyes in her mind.

"First day," she said out loud, making her voice low and smoky.

Haven dropped her hand and stepped back as the door to the office opened and Ethan walked out

Her eyes became hooded as she smelled the goodness of this one and it offended her. He reeked of it, making her want to hold her breath and growl in challenge.

Haven hid her hands in the folds of her skirt as her nails began to grow and the fingers wanted to twist into claws, her instinct to attack filling her until she could taste it on her tongue.

Ethan noticed the girl standing with his son and warning bells went off in his head. She looked like trouble. Glancing at his son, he recognized the glazed look of hunger in his eyes and knew, no matter what he said he would be seeing more of her.

"Thanks for coming in Mr. Goodwin," the secretary said, as she laid a comforting hand upon his back.

"Wyatt, why don't you show Miss Strange around today?" she asked, hoping it would keep him out of the office for a few days if he had something to do.

"We'll talk when you get home," Ethan said to his son's retreating back, receiving a wave of his hand in acknowledgement and dismissal.

"Well, good luck," Karen Dix offered again, as she too watched the school's brightest student, best athlete and biggest problem round the corner and disappear from sight.

Left standing alone in the hall as Ethan walked away, she wondered if she was going to have to notify maintenance of a lighting problem. She could have sworn that the hall became darker and the shadows deeper. Making a mental note to check on the situation later, she went back to her desk, blissfully unaware that the Dark had been let loose in her school and things were about to change.

The Dark flood gates had been opened, letting in a tidal wave of despair. After today no one would be safe.

No one.

Chapter 18

Wyatt waited outside the school's front doors after the last bell had sounded, hoping to catch Haven as she finished up her first day at his school.

He had done as asked and showed her around until there was nowhere else to explore. Leaving her at the door to her first class felt wrong to him, and he had been antsy and moody for the rest of the day.

He prowled the lunch room and the common area at lunch time, hoping to see her, but had come up empty, like his belly, since he had not taken the time to eat during his search.

He did not have a back pack slung over his shoulder or his arms filled to over flowing as every other student who exited the building did. He never had homework, finding the lessons easy and forever tedious.

He had a few minutes to kill before having to change and get out on the football field for practice, so he waited. His need to see her overrode his obligation to practice with the rest of the team. And even if he was a few minutes late, what were they going to do about it? Bench him? Not! His young, muscled shoulders carried the bulk of the team and their winning season on them.

So he leaned against the building and waited, only grunting as girls and boys filed passed and called out to him.

It made no impression on him that he was popular, but to be able to call him friend was a much coveted title in the social standing of his high school and the students worked hard for that honor.

He didn't care. He didn't need them or their petty drama to exist or be happy.

Well, that was not entirely true. He did find some measure of happiness when he sneered at the ones he considered lesser than himself. The ones whose families did not have the money to send them to school with the latest fashion. The ones who sucked at the sports he excelled in. The ones that had faces full of zits or the ones that cared nothing for life except what they could find in the books they always had their noses buried in.

They begged for his distain and he heaped it upon them, leading by example until the sheep that followed him picked up his cause and attacked like a hungry pack of wolves.

That made him smile. That seemed to calm the itch that lived inside him, making him twitchy and unsettled.

But only for a moment. Then it was back to itching and twitching.

As Wyatt waited for a glimpse of Haven, the twitch grew until he could hardly stand still.

The throngs of teens grew thin, and with it, his hopes of catching her before she went home. He did not take disappointment well.

When he had waited alone for five minutes with no one left to exit the school, Wyatt finally gave up. It was not with a shrug and a wistful feeling though. It was with anger and a teeth clenching growl that he headed for the locker room, carrying the small hope that knocking his teammates into the ground would give him some release.

Frustration fueled his movements and, in a short time, he walked out of the locker room door with his helmet under his arm. The shoulder pads he had put on made him look massive and the scowl on his face made him look mean. Mean enough that even the strongest of his teammates took one look at him, turned their backs and as one said "shit". They knew that look and it meant one thing, they were going to go home in pain. Again, "shit".

Wyatt took a deep breath and liked the smell of the freshly cut grass coming from the field.

He hefted his helmet and put it on, leaving the chin strap undone, before taking off in a trot to join his team in warm up.

He only made it two yards before a smoky voice hit his ears and his gut at the same time.

"What took you so long?" Haven asked, coming around the edge of the bleachers where she had been standing in the cool shadows.

"How did you know I'd be here?" Wyatt got out, willing to die before admitting he had been standing by the school's front door by himself looking for her.

"Kids talk," she said. "I listened. You're kind of a big deal around here aren't you?" she asked, not really caring about his answer, just wanting to see if she could make him squirm in false modesty.

The tall hunk of teenage masculinity didn't say a word, just shrugged those wide shoulders in indifference.

"Goodwin, get your ass out on the field!" a voice boomed, drawing everyone's attention to the couple standing by themselves.

Haven smirked as Wyatt's face turned pink and his lip curled at the interruption.

"Well?" Haven taunted. "Let's see what you've got," she said, flirting before turning to sit on the lowest bench, letting Wyatt know she was going to stay and watch.

Wyatt met her gaze for only a second before turning to lope across the field, where he was swallowed from sight by his team mates as they gathered around for a meeting.

He had no intention of putting on a show for the new girl. He didn't have to.

The itch that had made him want to grind someone, something into the ground was gone. For the first time for as long as he could remember, he felt settled, calm and for some strange reason, powerful.

He felt good.

Chapter 19

Haven stayed for the whole practice, watching with careful eyes as plays were run and different formations practiced and refined.

Time and again, she watched her target move with speed and grace as he mowed players over until he came at the ball carrier like a run away freight train, laying them out flat, leaving them gasping for air.

When Haven had been mortal she had never gotten into the sport of football. But now, as she carefully watched, she saw so much potential for trouble and pain to be added to the mix without causing any red flags to spring up, that she almost danced with excitement.

Her lips twitched and her nails dug into her palms each time the crack of helmets and pads echoed across the field. "*Ummmm,*" she purred to herself. She had a feeling she was going to like this assignment after all.

Being the good little minion of the Dark that she was, it did not take long before she noticed the players that sat or stood on the sidelines, not good enough to be allowed to play with the big boys.

Squinting her eyes to hide their truth, she allowed them to turn black before letting her mind reach out and worm its way into the fresh, young boys that stood or sat in rejection.

She probed and tasted each one until she found one ripe for her intentions. A small one that looked ridiculous in the oversized pads and the helmet that hid his fresh pink face from sight.

He ran up and down the sidelines, shouting encouragement to the ones on the field, acting like their own personal cheerleader because that was all he was good for.

Too small to play, so his butt warmed the bench game after game. Practice after practice, week after week, his role never changed. Even though he projected support and enthusiasm, Haven clawed out his true feelings until she knew his dark secret.

He envied what the others had, he resented not being allowed to play, and he hated not being a star and getting the recognition that came with it.

"You're never going to be good enough," Haven's mind whispered to his. *"Not just in these stupid sports, but all your life you will never be good enough".*

"Why even bother? No one notices you. No one cares if you are here or not. You are invisible to them, to everyone. Your parents are ashamed of the person you are. Never good enough for anyone or anything. Why bother? Why continue this farce called life?"

Haven sat back for a moment and considered if she should toy with him for a while longer or if she should just finish it here and now. Giving a slight shrug of her shoulders, she gave one last hard push before sitting back with a satisfied sigh.

She watched and listened as the boy's voice became silent and his shoulders sagged from the weight of despair.

She watched as he turned his back on the field and began walking back to the locker room, with steps that dragged with that same despair. No one noticed, no one cared.

As he passed her she saw, with her eyes of black, the chains that weighed him down and the smell of defeat was like perfume to her.

She stayed connected to him until he entered the deserted locker room. She waited until he took off his helmet, setting it aside carefully along with the rest of his gear before walking naked into the showers, turning on the hot water and ending his life with a razor from his duffel bag that he still had yet to use on his shiny clean face.

Haven watched the red run from his wounds and swirl until it disappeared down the drain, along with his young life.

She waited, still, until a Dark Minion rose from that same drain and collected the wailing spirit, dragging it screaming into the darkness below. Begging for another chance, regretting the actions he didn't know why he had taken.

Blinking her eyes back to human, Haven leaned back, smiling big. It really was like shooting fish in a barrel and she had accomplished it all without alerting the Guardian who was assigned to protect this weak one.

"Rah rah, yeah me!" she said, turning her attention back to her main objective.

Wyatt really was yummy, she decided, and she was definitely looking forward to tasting each morsel that she chewed off.

Yum!

Life was good.

Hunger was good.

And she was famished

Chapter 20

Wyatt took the helmet from his head and wiped the sweat from his eyes before making his way, with the others, towards the locker room. Practice was finished for the day and he was feeling good. Better than ever, in fact.

He had done all that was asked of him and more, never forgetting who watched him from the bleachers.

He slowed his steps as he pulled even with Haven and let the others pass by until they were alone.

The bright light of day had faded and the shadows, that now crept out to play, seemed cool and inviting. The lights that had come on during practice did not reach Haven and she sat in near darkness waiting for Wyatt to come to her.

He did.

When he stopped, Haven could feel the heat radiating from him and she smelled the sweat that was his scent on the night air.

She licked her lips in anticipation of what was to come.

"*About time!*" She thought as the first high pitched scream echoed through the empty halls of the school at her back.

She was okay with the fact the Wyatt left her side at a dead run to be swallowed up by the dark doorway that looked like a one-way portal to hell. At least to her it did. She liked it.

Gathering her things together, she left the school and the events that were unfolding inside. She had done what she wanted to today, so her time was now her own.

Her belly rumbled in human hunger and she let it dictate what was to come next. A big hamburger, fries and a strawberry milkshake seemed to be calling her name and she gladly gave in. It had been forever since she had eaten food and she looked forward to digging in now.

Haven opened her car door and slid behind the wheel, letting the dark and quiet wrap itself around her like a comforting blanket.

She sat in that dark and silence for a few moments with the feeling of coming home surrounding her before the oncoming sirens chased away her peace and made her drive away in the opposite direction.

She had fed her soul and now it was time to feed her human hunger. She had no need to stay and watch the mortals bring out their dead and wail in sorrow. She had seen it all a thousand times, caused it all a thousand times.

Whistling an eerie tune, she disappeared into the night, content to call it a day.

She did not worry about how Wyatt was handling the death of his team mate. No matter what he thought tonight, tomorrow she was going to make him like it.

Like it and want more.

Yup, burgers now she mused. Tomorrow was another day.

For her there would always be a tomorrow.

And another, and another and another…..

Chapter 21

Wyatt heard the screams and, without thinking, ran towards them.

When he reached the locker room he slowed until he came to a stop, taking in the scene playing out before him.

He watched as some of his team mates came running from the showers, dropping to all fours and puking where they landed. He watched others stagger out in shock and stumble, tripping over their downed friends, to land with wet splats on the cement floor. Still others ran slipping and sliding through the growing pools of stinking vomit, abandoned on the floor as the depositors slunk away, trembling and shaking from head to toe.

"Take a look," a voice urged in his head. *"You won't know what's going on if you don't grow a pair and go look."*

So he did, making his way around those still on the floor and the mess they and others had made.

Wyatt swallowed hard as he came to the doorway leading into the showers. The place where all the commotion seemed to stem from, before sucking in a breath and stepping in to see for himself what was going on.

He wasn't sure what he expected, but the sight in front of him was not even in the ballpark of what he would have imagined.

He had seen death before, living on a ranch as he did, but it was always animals that he had come in contact with. Never a human. Never someone he knew.

Not that he knew this boy well or anything. Hell, he couldn't even tell you his name if asked, but still it was a body he stared at, naked and pale, in its self-inflicted death.

Wyatt moved closer, his cleats echoing off the tiled walls as he put one foot in front of the other, until he stood before the wet body on the floor.

The water that still ran from above was no longer red, but still the pale pink told the tale of what had happened. That and the wide open cuts that marred each wrist, and of course, the razor lying loosely in a lifeless hand.

Wyatt reached out and turned the water off until nothing but the sound of a slow drip could be heard. He knelt down, leaning in close until his face was even with the dead kid's, trying to look into eyes that were only open to mere slits, trying to see what all the fuss was about. What death was about.

Naked lights shone on the white skin leaving nothing in shadow. Wet hair plastered the head, covering the eyes like bars on a jail cell and dripping water into the gaping mouth.

No secrets were whispered and no one jumped out screaming like in the horror movies he and his friends watched and laughed at. Nothing but stillness and dripping water could be heard until the coach came running in to push him aside screaming, "Someone call 911!"

"Too late for that," Wyatt sneered as he stood back, letting others make the calls and whatever else they were doing. Hurrying around, trying to think of something to do, when they might as well have just stopped and stayed still, was getting nothing accomplished. Nothing at all.

Chaos, shock and grief were the only things getting what they wanted for the next few minutes until uniformed men and women shoved their way into the showers and knelt over the white corpse.

Wyatt stepped back, seeing all he needed to, before changing his clothes, skipping the shower this time, and heading out to his pickup to go home.

Small knots of students, players, parents and looky-loos dotted the parking lot, all talking about or asking what had happened. He avoided them all, keeping his head down, letting them know he was not in the mood to share in the gossip.

Making it to his ride, Wyatt did not hesitate in climbing in and getting the heck out of Dodge. In no time at all he was out on the open road, all the traffic going towards where he had just left, so his way was clear and calm.

He rolled down his window to let in the cool night air, allowing it to ruffle his hair with massaging fingers that should have blown the stress away. Instead it seemed as if the breeze carried voices on it to his waiting ears. He listened to what it whispered, having no idea it was the Dark that came to him.

The voices blended with the whine of the tires, telling him over and over how the weak deserved no better than what the dead kid had gotten, an end to a life, putting them and others out of their misery.

It stroked Wyatt's ego, telling him how special he was and how he was destined for bigger things than living and dying in this pathetic little town.

Wyatt ate it up until he pulled into his own yard and killed the engine.

He sat and looked at the light beaming from the windows and wrinkled his nose as he remembered his father saying they were going to talk when he got home.

He was pretty sure that once he told his father what had happened after practice he would be off the hook for any lecture tonight.

As Wyatt swung his legs out, the voices slowed and quieted until there was only a low hum in his ears.

The black seed in his soul took huge bites of the darkness that now lay like a cloak upon his shoulders, gulping and swallowing until it became aware of danger.

Knowing it was not strong enough yet to meet an enemy, it crept slowly out until it peered through the human eyes of its host, content to just spy for now.

It saw what Wyatt could not, it smelled what Wyatt could not and it hated and growled as it saw the threat that Wyatt did not.

But it was safe for now, as Wyatt opened the door and passed through, closing it behind him. Shutting out the enemy.

In the cool night air, Gabriel rose from the crouch he had assumed when he sensed danger. His hair still stood on end and a deep rumble still rolled in his throat.

Mans best friend growled.

Callie hissed.

And everything changed.

Chapter 22

Wyatt had been right. Once he told his father what had happened at practice the talk that had been planned was put on the back burner and allowed to die a slow death.

Ethan went through the motions of fixing the evening meal for him and his son but, like every other parent in town, his mind was occupied with the why of what had happened.

Unlike his son, Ethan had known the now dead boy and, try as he might, he could find no clue as to why such a drastic measure had been taken.

He could not imagine having no recourse except to take your own life. Didn't Chester have friends he could have talked to? Ethan knew his parents and he knew they would have listened to anything their son would have talked to them about. They were good people, kind, solid and loving. So where had things gone wrong?

Fear, that if it happened once it might happen again and again until an epidemic of teen deaths rocked their small town, took root in his belly

Turning to his son, who for the most part had stayed quiet, Ethan found the courage to bring to light his hidden fear.

"You know?" he started and stopped. "You know," he tried again, "if you ever have a problem you can come to me right?" he asked, hoping his boy would be smart enough to get the jest of what he was beating around the bush at.

"Jeez dad," Wyatt said, rolling his eyes and beetling his brow. "I'm not going to jump off a cliff just because someone else did. Okay?"

"Something like this makes all parents stop and think." Ethan said, looking at his son. "I hope you know that you can always come to me if you want to talk or if you have troubles."

"I know that Dad," Wyatt said, seeing the love his father had for him in his eyes. "I can give you my word that if I ever have a problem I will come tell you."

"I know it's been kind of tough on both of us not having your mother here, but I will never let you down if you just come and talk to me," Ethan said, laying a hand on Wyatt's shoulder and squeezing it tight.

"Love you, too," Wyatt said, giving his father a strong hug for reassurance.

The Dark seed shrieked in pain as the love the human felt for its sire traveled throughout its body and left a warm glow behind.

The growth it had achieved that day was cut in half as it shrank from the goodness of the love the boy felt.

Gabriel, who had been let in earlier, forced his way in between the two men and with tongue lolling didn't budge until hands reached down and stroked his big head and soft body. He had been on guard, keeping watch ever since his young master had gotten home. The danger he had sensed was passed and he allowed himself to be stroked into pure bliss and doggie happiness.

Not so for Callie. She still rode the shoulder of her canine protector. She liked the happiness that radiated off him but she smelled the rot that grew inside this mortal, and it was bad. Deep down bad, she feared.

With arched back, Callie hissed out a warning, baring teeth that grew long and pointed. She may have been small but she was mighty, and she had friends in high places. And it was to those friends that she now called and summoned.

Gabriel stilled his wagging tail and cocked his massive head as he heard, with his canine ears, the rustling of wings outside the closed door. He listened and sniffed the air but, after a moment, went back to enjoying the stroking hands on his body as he detected no threat from the beings landing in the front yard.

The wind stirred and the earth groaned as one after the other hit the dirt from all directions.

In the blink of an eye Immortal Guardians filled the yard and stood as one, ready to do battle, answering the call for help from one of their own.

Callie joined them and stood in the center of the circle that they formed around her.

"Report!" Saul commanded, lifting a hand for Callie to sit upon, raising her up until she was eye level with those around her.

"Something has changed," she hissed, directing her comments to Saul, their leader.

"Go on," Saul said, knowing what she said was true. He could smell the residue of Dark from where he stood.

"When the boy came home today the dog and I could smell the scent of evil that walked with him," she started. "It is strong. Much stronger than when he left this morning. Something has changed!" she said again.

Ashton narrowed her eyes and, without a word, turned to enter the house and investigate Callie's claim.

She moved to where the dog lay and stroked a calming hand over the head he had lifted with her appearance. Assuring him of her good intentions until he once again rested that head on the pillow his paws formed.

Ashton moved to stand behind Ethan and heard his thoughts as he worried about the events that had happened this day. She gathered the information of the death of a young one and knew all he could supply her with before moving to stand beside Wyatt.

She smelled the rot coming from him and she clenched her hands in anger. Every morning she visited this mortal and pulled from his body and his mind the Darkness that grew there.

Every morning she departed, knowing she had not gotten it all, knowing she could not find the hidden seed that had taken root in this mortal. But sure that she had done enough to keep the Dark from taking over this boy.

But Callie was right. Something had changed. The Darkness she sensed now was big, bigger than any she had encountered from Wyatt before.

She stood by and read his thoughts, finding more information than Ethan could provide. Her eyes narrowed and her hands burned as she found the pleasure of the day's events buried in Wyatt's soul.

He liked what had happened. He thrilled in the blood and the death he witnessed. He cuddled this secret close to him and he stroked the feelings that he thought were his alone. Feelings of excitement and wonder.

Ashton sucked in a breath as she found the hunger that begged to be fed. As she watched, the hunger grew until it was ravenous and she grew fierce as the soul they were fighting for, the soul of Leonard, welcomed the hunger and Darkness as its master.

She hated being right. She hated that she had known this soul was sour from the beginning.

She withdrew to report back to the others and she heard the laughter the Dark taunted her with.

"No victory here." she whispered to the Dark that lurked all around.

"You have not won yet. Not yet!"

"Not yet!"

Maybe.

Chapter 23

Saul and the others watched as Ashton exited the human dwelling and he knew the news was bad as the fire in his friend burned, not just from her hands but engulfing her whole being.

Her fire burned bright in anger, causing the shadows that hid Dark spies to reveal their cloaked ones and send them moaning in pain back to the underground darkness. Back to Roman to report that the Guardians knew. Knew the time was ripe for the turning of Roman's pet soul. His obsession.

Ashton shared what she had found out with her friends and all were silent as they digested this information, trying to come up with a solution for the soul they fought for.

"What now?" Hunter questioned, being the first to speak.

All eyes turned to Saul for direction. All eyes carried the worry that, as a whole, they felt.

"We must continue to act as we have been," Saul advised. "We now know that the Dark has come out of hiding and has started its recruitment of Wyatt for the Dark side. We can do no more than fight to rid him of the evil trying to take control of his life."

Ashton pinched her mouth and narrowed her immortal eyes. She wanted more, more to be done to end this fight and save as many lives as they could.

"Its not enough!" she stated angrily, drawing all attention to herself. "Every day I have pulled the foul muck from his body and every day I find more than the day before to exterminate. There must be more we can do, more we can try. If we continue as we have been, we will lose!" she growled.

"Alright," Saul agreed. "What do you have in mind?"

Ashton hated to voice what she thought but her tongue would not be denied.

"I think we have no choice but to end this here and now!"

"Meaning?" Saul questioned, even though he knew what was coming.

"I think the only way to save this situation is to take the mortal life of Wyatt and send his soul on to its next level of existence. If we let things go, it may be too late to give his soul a chance at peace."

"If we do nothing the Dark will harvest this one and make it one of their own," she finished.

Saul glanced around the circle of Guardians and gauged their reactions to what Ashton had proposed. Some agreed, some questioned and some felt anger, but it would be his decision as to what would be done next. His was the final word.

Many times before he had opted for this course of action, taking the life of one to spare many, but he did not want to do it this time.

He wanted Leonard, or at least his soul, to have a chance to do good and be happy.

"Do any of you have more to say?" Saul asked, before giving his instructions.

Sam moved to stand behind Ashton, throwing his support behind her.

Jaxon and Hunter stood off to one side and, by their fierce looks, Saul knew they would like nothing more than to fight more of the Dark minions before admitting defeat.

Dee and Hannah stood as one, letting Saul see that they were not ready to give up and would fight to show Wyatt the path of goodness and happiness.

Still, Saul swung his eyes back to Ashton and Sam, knowing they were the ones that tried to kill the Darkness within Wyatt every morning. Taking the sadness from Ethan's heart and allowed him to live without his soul mate day after day.

These two were the closest to the situation and Saul valued their opinion, but he would not admit defeat. Not just yet.

"I can see in your eyes what each of your decisions are," Saul began. "I know what each of you feels and I can relate to those feelings, but I will ask you all to not give up on this one. This soul that deserves to be happy and find the path destiny has written for it."

"So we fight?" Jaxon asked, a spark igniting in his dark eyes.

"Yes," Saul said with conviction. "We fight!"

No matter what each wanted, they would follow Saul's directions until the fight was won and the Dark moved on or until the Dark won and evil chaos was let loose.

"We will continue as we have with Sam and Ashton doing what they can to keep Wyatt and his father safe." Saul continued.

"Jaxon and Hunter will stay close and dispatch all the Dark Ones that make the mistake of coming here to spy and cause mischief. Dee and Hannah will watch over the town and alert us if any more of the young ones are swayed to follow the path the one known as Chester chose today."

"And me?" Callie asked.

Saul reached out his hand and stroked the soft fur, bringing the little protector close to his chest.

"You, little one, will continue to watch over these mortals and raise the alarm when trouble comes to call." Saul said in a comforting tone. "And it will." Saul thought. It would come to call and want to move in permanently.

Saul hoped his decision was sound and all would end in their favor. But the worm of doubt was alive and well in his heart and it was growing.

All he would allow himself, at this time, was to watch and aid his warriors as the lines of battle were drawn and both sides dug in for the long haul.

He was not above praying for help, but the Fates were silent as they watched from afar and clutched each other in sorrow.

The price Saul was to pay for this soul would be high.

High and steep.

But they could not interfere.

Chapter 24

Ashton stood by the bed of Wyatt and watched as the soft morning light kissed his face with beauty and calm. Making it hard to believe one who looked so innocent and good could be harboring the Darkness they fought.

Early morning was when she tasked herself with pulling as much corruption from this body as she could reach. Each morning she moved away, knowing her efforts were not enough.

She did not like coming up short and having to taste the bitterness of defeat each day, leaving her growling and unsatisfied.

Grinding her teeth in determination, Ashton once again laid her hands on Wyatt's chest and watched as they disappeared, allowing her to feel for the Darkness that played hide and seek with her.

"Come here you little bastard!" she spit out, as her hands found the hard knots of blackness and burned them with fingers that cleansed with fire.

She fought for every bit she took until she could feel no more. She couldn't feel it but she sensed there was more hiding from her. She just couldn't find it.

As she pulled her hands back, tendrils of blue fire still held her connected to the human, until she straightened fully and, with a soft pop, they let loose and disappeared.

"Well?" Sam asked, placing his hands on her tense shoulders.

"The crap is still there!" Ashton said, spitting the foulness from her mouth.

"He would have been lost almost from birth if not for the work you do every day," Sam soothed, as he gently pulled her close to his side.

"We can only do so much and hope that as the spirit of those we try to save grows stronger with age, they will be able to rid themselves of the last little bit we cannot reach," Sam lectured from his heart.

"Don't hold your breath on this one," Ashton ground out, as she stared at the teen sleeping so peacefully before her.

"This one is going bad fast!" she admitted to Sam alone.

"Why didn't you tell Saul this yesterday?" Sam wanted to know, a frown of concern marring his handsome brow.

Ashton shrugged her wing ridden shoulders before crossing her arms and answering with the truth.

"This one is special to Saul" she began. "I don't know why it is, but it just is. Because of this, I try not to put a damper on it and he thinks I may be a little prejudiced because of what Leonard did to us, taking away our mortal future and all."

Sam knew exactly what she meant because he too had the urge to wring the little turd's neck on more than one occasion because of what was stolen from him. But he tried to be the bigger man and let it go. In his mortal life Sam would have taken Leonard out and dusted his hands off when finished. No regrets no nightmares, no worries.

Things were different now. Now he fought for the side of good and, if it wasn't for Ashton, he would have teamed up with Jaxon and Hunter, kicking up his heels as he delivered death sentences to the Dark Ones he hunted.

Just thinking about it made him want to prowl the shadows and taste again the sweetness of dealing out justice to those he got paid to send on, to put it nicely. Or if you like, murdered. What ever way you looked at it, Sam had been good at his job in life and, in death, would have been a deadly asset to the Guardians.

Ashton meant more to him though than that, so he dialed it down and did what he could with the restrictions he imposed upon himself.

Wiping a hand across his face, Sam erased those feelings and once again turned his attention to his partner.

"I still think it would be a good idea to warn Saul and the others about what is coming down the pike," he said, hoping she would not take offense to his seeming to back the others instead of her.

"Very well," Ashton sighed, caving to his suggestion.

Taking Sam's hand, Ashton stepped back, preparing to turn Wyatt's care back over to Callie and her mortal companion.

Before she left, she turned one more time to stare at her failure.

Letting out a gasp, she stopped, drawing Sam's attention to first her and then to the bed that held her gaze.

Ashton stood as still as stone, surprised to see Wyatt's eyes opened and searching the room until they found what they were looking for.

Gone were the beautiful, bright, blue eyes of a human. And in their place were the flat, black, lifeless marbles that gave evidence to the Dark in residence.

Tan skin turned ashen and the smile that spread across the mouth showed teeth jagged and grey with decay.

Sam yanked Ashton away, until she finally blinked her eyes again.

"We have to go now," he said to her, pulling her behind him to protect her.

As they unfurled their wings and gave a mighty leap into the air, Ashton was sure she heard the gravely sound of a laugh behind her, until an icy chill caught up to her and ran a cold finger down her spine.

"Come back and play," the wind in her ears whispered, making her dig deeper with each stroke of her fiery wings.

"You can run from me," the Dark whispered "but sooner or later sister, we're going to dance. You and me, we're going to dance!"

The dark laughed.

Chapter 25

Wyatt woke not long after Sam and Ashton had departed, having no memory of the events that had taken place or the voice that had threatened Ashton through him.

All he knew was he felt rested and actually looked forward to starting his day.

He took a few moments to relax with his hands behind his head, letting his mind wander until it found the memory of a dream he had had the night before.

His eyes closed as he let the dream once again wash over him, through him. He remembered seeing Haven in a dark forest, standing in the deep shadows and not caring that her eyes glowed red with hell fire and smoked with a message of lust and dark passion. She wanted him to join her, be with her, here in the dark that surrounded them.

Wyatt drank in the sight of her body, eerily glowing pale and ashen in the dark, and thrilled as his body came alive with want and desire.

He stepped closer and let his hands reach out to brush her dark hair back over her shoulders until the treasures it was hiding fed his hungry eyes.

Soft young breasts lifted and pointed with each breath she took, inviting him to reach out and cup them in his eager hands. He did. The feeling of flesh in his palms was not new to him but the feeling of her flesh was.

Before, he had taken what was offered to him by the girls in his town, with the grunts and groans of a normal teenage boy, but with Haven it was different.

The mounds he now held in his hands did not seem warm and soft. Instead he felt a coldness travel from his hands until goose bumps jumped from his body, causing the hardness between his legs to grow even larger. He felt power in his erection and he wanted to drive it deep into her until he made her squirm and scream with pleasure and pain at his hugeness.

He moved to join himself with her but was held back as her hands reached out to touch his body and fan the flames that already licked at his skin.

It was not a hot flame that scorched his body, but rather an icy fire that seeped deep into his bones and engulfed him until he was almost mad with wanting her.

He heard her laugh in the darkness and he saw long grey teeth in her open mouth before she knelt down in front of him, and he could do nothing but grab onto her hair as her mouth closed around him.

He tried to move in that mouth, to force her to take more, but razor sharp points bit down and he stilled with the pain. He liked it. He let her have her way.

His eyes could not see in the deep blackness, so he closed them and let his senses tell him what was happening, what she was doing.

The tongue that swirled around him, and the lips that smacked as she moved, made all the other fumbling experiences he had had disappear from his memory, until there was only this time, this girl, this feeling left.

He wanted to slide down until he had her under him but she pushed him backwards, until he felt tree bark bite into his skin and reveled in the power she held over him.

He never saw, in the blackness of night, the nails that grew from her hands and feet until sharp claws gouged deep holes in the tree allowing her to climb until her breasts touched his open mouth. Until the wetness between her legs demanded he enter and fill her, as she opened herself to him.

His breath came heavy through his nose as he filled his mouth with her, sucking her in, wanting to taste and feed like a baby at its mother's breast. Only his suction was strong and the pull on her made her fling back her head until Wyatt could feel her long hair as it touched and clung to the dewy droplet at the end of his shaft.

He raised his hands until he cupped her sweet checks and pulled to spread her open. Hearing her gasp, as he pushed upward, made him feel like he had been struck by lightning and the current of electricity sizzled through his body, making him hum everywhere.

He dug deep for control and deeper into her, until their combined wetness ran down his legs and washed his feet.

He stood panting, grateful for the tree that held him up or he would surely have fallen to the ground.

His legs felt like water and he trembled with the release of passion, like none he had ever known before. Then nothing.

Wyatt came back to himself as he lay sweating and panting on his bed, in his room, alone.

He swallowed to wet the dryness in his mouth and his throat before pulling his hands from behind his head. He clasped them across his body and was surprised to find streaks of wetness splashed on his belly and up his chest.

Rather than be embarrassed, Wyatt reached down and fiddled with his now soft member, making it a promise that the next time, the next time would be for real.

Soon, he promised himself as he swung his legs over the side of the bed and headed for the bathroom.

Real soon.

Chapter 26

Haven sat up in her bed, hot, sweaty and panting for human breath. The dream she had given Wyatt was more than accepted by him and, as he was a willing participant, Haven had gotten more than she had bargained for.

She had figured she would have to coax and lead him where she wanted him to go, but he had taken charge and both had gotten lost in the forbidden dream.

It was widely unacceptable to have such self satisfying dreams, but Haven needed to give him a taste of what they could mean to each other.

Wyatt never noticed or questioned the way her skin had glowed an eerie grey, or the way she had shimmied up the tree until she was positioned to receive him. Her claws had dug into the tree, turning it black with death. But in a dream, who really cared about such things? Right? Not Wyatt! His eyes had been glazed or closed so she did what she wanted without detection.

Haven gave a deep sigh as she stretched before rising from the dirty bed she had slept in.

Finding somewhere to live had presented a problem, until she remembered seeing a run down shack set far back from a dirt road in the middle of nowhere. Finding and taking that turn, she had been more than satisfied with her new abode. No one would come looking for adventure here, and if they did, she had some nasty surprises up her sleeve that would send them running in fear.

Haven stood in the bathroom with its cracked mirror and its filthy tub and sink, but she didn't care. The water she needed came to her when she passed a hand over the facets and the creaking groans of the pipes reminded her of home. Ah, music to her ears!

She had no need to have a place to hang extra clothing, as she changed her wardrobe at will, with nothing more required than a thought from her head.

She washed her body and called up a hot wind to dry her skin and hair before opting for more black clothes to begin her school day with.

Looking at her reflection, she approved of the black leggings that hugged her legs and the soft black sweater that was long enough to cover her butt but dipped low enough in the front to show some young cleavage.

A dark belt rode low on her hips and glittered in the dim light. The stupid human children would think it a pretty bauble, but she knew the stones were really black diamonds found in the pits of the place she knew as home.

Finishing her look with low leather boots, she was ready to go.

Her stomach gave a deep growl, reminding her that she had one more thing needing to be taken care of. Hunger.

She could always eat the vermin that shared her bed, but her mouth began to water as she imagined the pleasure of biting into a giant, gooey cinnamon roll.

She wiped her chin of the wetness that ran from her mouth before heading out the door and into town for her treat.

Pulling up to the local store, she sat and waited until a man pulled in beside her before she got out and stood before him.

"Money," she said in a whisper and, holding out her hand, did not withdraw it until he had placed several bills in it.

She walked away, leaving him scratching his head and wondering why he was just standing in the parking lot instead of going inside.

Her choice for breakfast did not disappoint, and she even remembered to grab some junk food for her lunch before heading to school and her target.

Haven wondered if Wyatt would act different after the dream he had had, but no matter. She would make sure he thought of little else in his free time.

She pulled into an out of the way parking spot, turned off the motor and sat licking the tasty goo from her fingers before gathering her things and climbing out.

The still early morning shadows hugged the trees and, as she passed them by, her eyes easily picked out the dark forms hiding amongst them.

Letting her eyes go black, she growled low in her throat, warning them away from her territory.

"Back off!" she warned. She was not above dispatching one of her kind if they dared to cross her and most of them knew it, scattering like good little rats before a flood.

She wasted no more time on them, as the hair on the back of her neck stood up. She sensed her prey approaching and smirked in pleasure before walking in a straight path towards the open doors.

"Catch me if you can," she sang under her breath, as she swung her hips with each step.

She dangled the bait before hungry eyes and scented the air with dark musk, assuring Wyatt's attention was fixed on her and her alone, before being swallowed up by the maw of the human school.

She was now on the clock and anticipated the cat and mouse game she would play with Wyatt.

And before he could have a chance to be saved by his Guardian he would find out just what kind of kitty she really was.

A monster.

Chapter 27

Wyatt's days fell into a routine, with him chasing Haven through the halls of school during the day, and through his dreams at night. Not every night, thank God, or else he would have had his brain fried from the heat they generated as they came together in the dark.

Every day he looked for her, trying to get her alone, so he could have a chance to ask her out. But every day he was left with frustration and nothing more. No date, no flirting, nothing to ease his pain except the dreams he conjured a couple of times a week.

As hot as those dreams were, he wanted her in the flesh, in his arms, in his bed. Not in his imagination.

He thought they had gotten along pretty well that first day and because of his reputation of the "it" guy in school and the whole town, he had been sure he could get her without breaking a sweat. But, as he found out, his popularity got him nowhere when it came to claiming her for his own. Things had changed.

There had been no more deaths among the young but, unless one paid attention, the hidden hints of chaos could easily be missed. And for the most part they were.

Petty vandalism was on the rise, along with drinking, drugs, and assaults. The parents and those older just put it down to kids acting like the spoiled rotten little creeps they were, never seeing the big picture.

If they had looked deeper the alarm would have been raised and steps taken to restore order. Maybe even to the extent that Haven's plans, influence and maybe even she herself, would have been squashed like the disease ridden cockroach she was. But no one added up the incidents. No one looked at the big picture, and no one lifted a finger to stop what was building.

It wasn't until after the first home football game that Wyatt finally found a chance to talk to Haven alone.

The crowd had been wild when their team pulled off a close win and many rushed the field when the final gun sounded and the game was over.

Wyatt received slaps on the back from the men, each secretly wishing it had been them to win the game, and kisses and hugs from the females, old and young alike, as he stood with his team mates basking in the glory of victory.

His smile was huge as sweat dripped from his hair, even though the night was cool and the nip of winter was in the air. He had played hard and he had played well, leaving two players from the other team benched and on their way to the doctors when they got home.

Victory was sweet and he drank it in, knowing he had done the work of three and liking the pain he could cause, all under the guise of playing a game.

Ethan stood back on the side lines, not wanting to fight the crowd around his son, biding his time until Wyatt came to him and shared a moment alone to talk and get a hug from him. That was their ritual. That was something special they had always shared. Always.

Until tonight that is, something changed and unlike all the others in town, Ethan felt it. He saw it. He knew something was wrong.

As he stood by himself, he felt a frigid wisp of cold air surround him and bite at his exposed flesh and he frowned.

He stood still, trying to figure out what was up, until he caught a movement out of the corner of his eye. He turned his head ever so slightly and watched as the girl he had seen in the hall a while back passed close by him on her way out to the field.

He rubbed his eyes as the light around her seemed to dim and the cold too receded as she got farther away with each step she took. "*How could that be?*" he wondered to himself, not liking what he was thinking.

Ethan was not one to believe in demons and such, but as he sucked in a breath and blew out vapors, he couldn't help but think the unthinkable.

He watched as Haven stopped at his son's side and, as impossible as it seemed, the darkness moved and stopped with her.

The two were but dim figures as they talked with heads close together, almost touching, but not quite.

Ethan doubted what his eyes were seeing and he wondered what to do, who to tell, or even what to tell.

"Oh say Chuck, did you notice how it gets really cold when that new girl walks by? Oh, and do you notice how she seems to suck the light out of the air and things get dark around her?"

Ethan ran the conversation around in his head, testing it out, and each time he tweaked it, it still sounded like he was crazy and or delusional. Who was going to believe him when he told them he thought she was a demon from hell?

As he stood and watched his heart broke just a little, as Wyatt and Haven walked off the field together and his son never even glanced his way. He had been forgotten.

He got a taste of how it felt to be discarded, forgotten and he was not ready for it.

As he gulped back the feelings that tightened his chest he happened to see Haven glance over her shoulder and lock her gaze with his.

The smile that she flung his way was riddled with contempt and, as that smile turned into a sneer, Ethan could have sworn she had stuck her tongue out at him.

"But how could that be?" he wondered. Because the thing that came out of her mouth was long and black and, where the spit dripped from it, the grass hissed before turning black and dying.

Ethan stumbled back and would have fallen had Sam and Ashton not caught him from behind.

Ashton threw a look to Sam, making sure he had Ethan under control, before she leapt into the air and shot like a bullet towards the being that held Wyatt's arm in her grasp.

It looked like a human girl but Ashton could smell and see the Darkness and she meant to do it harm.

She meant to kill it!

Chapter 28

Sam watched, with his hands on Ethan, as his soulmate flew to do battle with the Dark alone. Foolishly alone.

To the mortal eye Wyatt and Haven seemed to be the only ones left on the football field. But that was not true. The Dark Minions that lurked in the night shadows were many. As Ashton neared one of the Dark's own, they gave up their hiding places and poured out in boiling waves, to stand between their Dark One and the fiery Guardian.

The football field had been transformed into a battle field and, with the odds in the Dark's favor, Ashton did not stand a chance.

With a silent command from his Guardian, Ethan turned and left without a backward glance, freeing Sam to fight by Ashton's side.

As mighty as these two Guardians were, still two against so many would guarantee the Dark a victory.

Sam slammed into the wall of Darkness, cutting a wide path, sending black blood spewing into the night. He called for help as he fought his way towards the white hot column of flames that showed him where Ashton did battle with the enemy.

Before he could reach her the earth moaned and the winds screamed with the arrival of warrior Guardians Jaxon, Hunter, Dee and Hannah.

No words were needed as each could see the reason they had been called for aid.

Razor sharp wings and fiery blades were swung through the air, cutting a wide swath as each of the Guardians fought to reach Sam and Ashton.

Jaxon gave a mighty cry as he sliced and diced the flood of Dark that came for him. His face was grim as he gave no quarter to his enemy and he felt nothing but pleasure as smoke rose from the piles of black bodies he had cut to ribbons in his wake.

Hunter too fought, but he stayed close to Dee and Hannah, as they made their way to the center of the fray.

As each Guardian arrived, they took their place until a circle was formed and protection was given to backs that the Dark were prone to attack.

As humans began to filter out of the school, they ran for their cars, hearing what they thought was thunder. But in reality it was the battle that took place right under their mortal noses.

The fog that lay like pea soup on the ground was not fog at all, but smoking vapor each dead Minion emitted as it was dispatched by the protectors of humanity.

For every Dark One that the Guardians put down, two more took its place, until a black sea rolled and crashed, surrounding the warriors leaving no path for escape.

No escape until a bolt of lightning struck the field, so bright that the lights winked out and the ground shook with the force it generated.

It was no ordinary display of Mother Nature's wrath, but the arrival of Saul, as the light he carried and the power that was his, wiped out all the Dark that was foolish enough to threaten his friends.

Saul stood like a beacon and his warriors came to him, covered in blood and grime, while the last of the Dark escaped into the night, fleeing before the might of the most feared Immortal Guardian of them all.

"Speak!" Saul commanded, as his hair flew around his face and the light of battle still burned in his eyes.

Ashton stepped forward, still breathing hard, the fire she still felt flickering in her emerald eyes, to speak as commanded.

"The Dark, it seems, have taken a page from our book," she said, while her eyes cut sideways to land on Hunter. "They have sent a Dark One back in human form, a female, to influence Wyatt to join Roman's army."

"I believe this is why I have not been able to stop the Dark from spreading so quickly in Wyatt lately. We will have to come up with a plan to counter this one's power over the human or he will be lost," she said, falling silent with the others.

Saul cocked an eyebrow, preparing to speak, but before he could Wyatt and Haven stepped out of the school into the dark night. What he saw confirmed Ashton's assessment of the situation, for his eyes stripped away the guise of humanity and saw the demon beneath.

He saw the blackness inside and how that evil smirked, knowing they could not attack while Wyatt was right beside her.

Saul looked inside the boy and again saw darkness inside him, but not all consuming, as it was with the girl. There was still a chance for this soul to be saved. But it would take work and vigilance to pull it off.

That and a really good plan.

Saul let a smile creep out and light his face, causing the Dark One to take a step back, and he enjoyed wiping the smirk from her black lips.

"Follow me," he said to his friends. "You're right Ashton," he grinned, leaping into the air to lead them away. "I do have a plan and I think you're going to like it."

Saul disappeared from sight, but left a laugh of pure joy trailing behind him.

Haven heard and her skin crawled with the feeling she had that he laughed at her expense.

The time of hiding was over.

She was exposed.

Chapter 29

"Turn her!" Saul said, staring at Ashton.

"Excuse me?" Ashton questioned, her eyes going round in disbelief.

"Turn her," Saul said again, this time smiling into all the eyes that blinked at him.

"It will be the last thing Roman and his followers will be expecting. They will assume that we will come at them, and the girl, with the intentions of eliminating her and all the others that they would send after her."

"If they think we are going soft and cannot accomplish this, they will not stray from their plan and we will have a chance to turn the tables on them." Saul finished, giving the bare essentials of what he thought should come next.

"This does not mean that we will stop fighting them in the open though," he continued. "To do so would arouse their suspicions and the plan would fail before it got started."

"Not only will we deprive Roman of Leonard's soul, we will also take from him an obviously trusted follower," Saul pointed out to his skeptical audience.

Jaxon and Hunter leaned back on the rocks of the mountain top where they sat and both turned the idea over in their minds until, sharing a look, they nodded their heads in agreement.

"Tell us what you want us to do," Jaxon spoke for both of them.

Saul spent the rest of the dark hours, until the sun began to rise, going over what he wanted each to do. Listening to their ideas as they hashed out the finer points of the plan he had come up with.

Before they went their separate ways, each knew the role they were to play and how they were to proceed.

It was a good plan and a daring one, sure to tweak the nose of the Dark Leader, but it just might work.

Turning one from the Dark Side was almost impossible but Saul had chosen this course of action for just that reason.

His warriors were strong and he had to have faith that they would succeed before their actions were detected. If they were found out, it would be all out war, as he was sure Roman would be furious at their trying to steal one of his own and reclaiming one he dearly wanted.

Saul stood alone for a moment, taking in the beauty of the mountain vista that lay at his feet, before spreading his wings. With one mighty leap he took to the air to soar over the peaks and valleys that gave peace to his spirit.

He drank in that peace until he was calm and filled with as much energy as the Earth could give him, before banking and heading to watch over his friends.

As he disappeared from sight the Fates whispered to each other and those whispers carried on the gentle wind that blew through silent tree tops and tickled the tufts of hardy grass.

They whispered their concern at what was to come until the winds moaned with their warnings and the trees bent to their power.

A storm was born and it was all powerful carrying on its back the promise of death and an ending to come.

But it kept the secret of whose.

Chapter 30

Ashton spent the night by Wyatt's side, taking her time, searching for all the Dark she could find and turning it to ash with her hands of white hot fire.

She probed and dug until her shoulders ached with her efforts, but she didn't call it quits until the sun sent a rosy glow filtering in through the curtained windows. The shadows that had been with her during the night receded, until they were forced to disappear and give way to the light, leaving the promise of a new day in their wake.

Sam had stood by her side as she worked, giving Ashton his protection from the Minions that appeared with the setting of the sun. More than one had been promptly dispatched as they foolishly grew bold and dared to threaten her safety.

Sam made sure they died in silence, never getting the chance to tell the tale of what the Guardians were up to.

No longer did Ashton wait until the morning light to rid the young mortal of his Darkness and she now had others at her side as she worked.

As the light grew stronger, Sam folded his wings, heaved a sigh and relaxed his vigil. It had felt good to attack the fleas that lived in the night and send them on to nothingness. He smiled in satisfaction.

"Are you gloating?" Ashton teased, coming to his side as she flicked the last ashes from her now normal hands.

"Why yes, I believe I am," Sam said, letting his smile grow into a bright grin.

"Duh," Dee said, as she joined them at the foot of Wyatt's bed. She had spent the night connected to Wyatt's mind and had made sure no dreams the Dark sent to him could get through.

Instead, she opened his mind and let memories of the good times spent with his father surface and be relived.

Dee let him taste the sweetness of the love he felt for his father until it filled his dreams and his being, driving back into hiding the seed Roman had planted in his soul at birth.

She had blanketed the moans of its pain so no others could hear until they had died down to mere whimpers of despair.

Dee had tried to push it into the open for Ashton to destroy, but it was sly and hid so she could not find it either. She had been unsuccessful, but she felt fine with her night's work and nodded her head in her own satisfaction.

It wasn't long before Hunter joined them and the four stood talking quietly about their roles and how each had fared.

Hunter nodded his head at what was being said, but his eyes traveled the room seeking his friend and partner.

"I'm here," Jaxon said, being one of the last to arrive. He had spent the night traveling the town and the ranch, seeking out any Dark Ones that came poking around, looking for humans that were alone and easy prey.

"Where's Hannah?" Jaxon asked, looking to Hunter for answers as he had been assigned her protector in this endeavor.

"Right behind me," Hunter supplied, but he did not expect the hand that reached out and grabbed him by the shoulder in anger.

"You were supposed to stay with her and guard her!" Jaxon spit out, while drawing his friend in close. "Not leave her until she was with the rest of us, remember?" Jaxon growled, ready to punish Hunter if anything happened to Hannah.

"Relax Jaxon," a quiet voice sounded at his back. "I'm fine," Hannah said, the softness of her voice telling the others that the task assigned to her had left her tired and drained.

Jaxon dropped his hand from Hunter's shoulder as he turned to gather his mate to his side.

"You were supposed to stay with Hunter," Jaxon chided her, as relief coursed through his powerful body. "What happened?"

Hannah rolled her eyes and shook her head at Jaxon's protective attitude, but she was glad that he cared for her the way he did.

The love they had found as humans carried over into this existence and burned strong in both of them. She could not fault him for the way he reacted to her absence.

But still she would not have him place blame where it was not due.

"It took me a while to find this Dark One in human form, but it all went as planned," she said, as the Guardians gathered around her to hear what she had to say.

"Hunter kept the others occupied while I snuck in and did a little exploring," she said, throwing a wink in Hunter's direction.

"I just went a ways away and sent out an invitation for any in the area to come and get me," Hunter supplied, catching an elbow in the ribs from Dee for the risk he had taken.

"Show off!" Dee said, sharing a look with Hannah as each knew how the other felt, being in love with a fierce fighter that took risks and denied any fear.

"Let's continue this somewhere else," Jaxon said, as Wyatt stirred in the bed, preparing to wake up.

Six sets of magnificent wings opened and prepared to carry them away. But before they left Dee crept quietly over to the bed and placed a hand on Wyatt's head. Bending down close to his ear, she whispered words that took root in his heart and warmed his soul.

"Remember," she said softly. "Remember all the good in your life and the ones that love you. Fight! Fight for them!" With her final words, Dee leaned over and placed a soft kiss on his cool brow, sealing in her words and allowing them to take root. It was all she could do for now until sleep once again came to him and she could work with Ashton to claim this soul.

Sam clasped Ashton's hand as, two-by-two, the other Guardians followed them to meet where they would not disturb the humans.

All was not revealed yet and blanks needed to be filled in.

For now, Wyatt was safe. As safe as they could make him.

But it had only just begun.

Chapter 31

Six sets of immortal feet landed with a boom that echoed off their favorite mountain tops. It set birds to flight as the winds whipped the towering pines into a frenzy with their arrival.

"Should we wait for Saul?" Dee asked, finding a soft bed of moss to rest upon.

"I called to him but he is tied up right now and said he would join us when he could," Jaxon provided, taking the position of lead in Saul's absence.

"Very well," Hannah said, clearing her throat as she began to relate what she had found.

"I found the Minion that Roman sent after Wyatt," she began. "I waited until this thing lay down to rest and, being pretty damn sneaky if I do say so myself, I was able to get inside her and look around."

"What did you find?" Jaxon asked, wanting to know what they were up against.

"I think we have a chance," Hannah said, letting a small smile curve her pretty lips. "While it is true that this being is Dark, I was able to find one small spark of light still living deep in her heart and I think we can clear a path for it and help it to grow."

Five pairs of eyes stared at Hannah until the spark of hope she felt began to burn inside her friends. Each Immortal mind was busy thinking of what their role would be in helping this dim glimmer of hope grow until it would be a power that could drive out the Dark imbedded within Haven and allow the Guardians to turn her towards the light.

Hannah's blood red eyes glowed with hope as she described how she had chipped away at the Darkness, leaving the fragile light a greater space to breathe and grow.

"I could tell when you made the hole," Dee spoke up, drawing eyes to her as she began to speak. "I connected with Haven's mind, while Ashton worked on Wyatt, and was able to bring forth some happy memories for her to relive and find pleasure in. She has few to choose from, but anything is a good start. Maybe, as Hannah works, I will be able to dig deeper and find more memories to add some fuel to the fire to feed our hope."

The tension that had held the group in thrall relaxed its grip and allowed them all to breathe a little easier as plans formed in their minds and ideas grew strong.

"I think Jaxon and I will continue our hunting and provide protection for you and Hannah," Hunter offered, waiting for and receiving an agreeing nod from Jaxon.

The look Jaxon threw at Hunter let him know he had not forgotten Hunter had arrived before Hannah and if it happened again he, Jaxon, would be having a little heart to heart with his fellow Guardian.

Hunter smirked as Hannah caught that same look and did not hesitate in letting Jaxon know her feelings as a low growl vibrated in her throat.

"Dee and I can protect each other," Hannah said, looking straight at Jaxon. "If we need help we are very well versed in opening our mouths and asking for it."

Dee giggled and sat up a little straighter to see what fireworks Hannah's words would cause in Jaxon. Her laughter grew a small amount as she watched the Immortal's lips press tight and his eyes go hooded.

"Before this gets out of hand," Ashton said, butting into the conversation "I think we all have a pretty good idea what needs to be done and who needs to do what. Let's all just focus on that."

Shoulders relaxed and tension eased as Jaxon finally huffed out a sigh and backed down from his self-appointed roll of Hannah's protector.

"Thank you," Hannah said, as she looped her arm around her mate's waist and gave it a loving squeeze.

"Dee and I will continue to work on Haven while Jaxon and Hunter do some damage to the Dark Ones that are still lurking around," Hannah spelled out so all were clear on how to proceed.

"Ashton and I will stick with Wyatt and Ethan during the daylight hours," Sam added. "I think if we can keep both feeling positive and good we can make this Haven's job much, much harder."

"We will pop in several times a night and keep the dreams working in our favor. We just have to make sure the Dark does not wonder why we are putting in more time with this mortal than is normal for us." Sam finished.

"I think Jaxon and I can keep them busy enough that they will not have time to wonder why the Guardians are being extra vigilant," Hunter threw in.

Jaxon agreed and both Guardian hunters ruffled their wings in anticipation of the battles to come.

Ashton planned on cleansing Wyatt every night and sticking close every day. So her time would be spoken for until this assignment was completed, one way or the other.

"Such trouble!" she thought to herself as she stood alone, watching her friends with their heads together. The arms she held crossed in front of her chest hugged tighter as her buried feelings of resentment nibbled at their confines, trying to get loose.

Ashton never let on that lately she had been having trouble feeling sorry for the soul of Leonard. If it was so hot-to-trot to side with the Dark then why not just let it and kill it when it did?

Ashton blinked her emerald eyes and shook her head to dispel the thoughts that wanted to leave a bitter taste in their wake.

"Sam?" Ashton said, reaching out a hand in invitation. "Can we go now? Everyone and everything seems to be in order so how about it?"

Sam gladly took her hand and, clasping it tight in his own, they made their farewells, and in less than a minute they were gone.

Hannah took a step away from Jaxon's side and watched the two as they grew smaller with the distance they put between themselves and their group of warriors. Her eyes glowed like fire as she sensed something off, but the feeling seemed to ebb to nothingness as they faded from sight

Hannah stood quietly, deep in thought, until Jaxon came to her side and they prepared to leave together. She did not forget her feeling of unease, but instead filed it away until she was in Ashton's presence again. Only then would she be able to tell if what she sensed was still there, or if Ashton had been able to rid herself of whatever it was that Hannah had detected.

Taking their leave left only Dee and Hunter standing alone, the last to depart.

"What do you think so far?" Dee asked her mate now that they were alone and could speak freely.

"I think we have a chance," Hunter said with conviction, as he gently lay his lips on the top of Dee's head and gave her a kiss for reassurance. "I don't think we will be defeated in this quest if we stand as one."

Dee gave a sigh of relief as she drank in Hunter's confidence and made it her own. She nodded her head and, opening her wings, gave a leap into the air to speed away with Hunter by her side.

The Window to the World would give them a chance to spy and see for themselves if they had done any good the night before. If not, they would have to try something else.

Only time would tell.

Chapter 32

Roman knew what he had known all along, that the Guardians tried every night to rid the human, known as Wyatt, of the Dark seed he had planted in his soul the day of its mortal birth.

Roman knew that with the dawning of each new day the Guardians came up short and it made him snicker in glee. It wasn't often that he could count a victory when Darkness was detected in a human being.

Most times the Guardians were able to pull it out by the roots and vanquish it. Most times.

A few special mortals had been able to hold on to the Dark and grow in its shadow, until the evil matured and mankind felt the power the Dark was able to wield. Those were the ones Roman pampered and took to his side when death scraped them from the Earth, only to have them rise up again, more powerful in death than they could have imagined in life.

These were the Dark Ones he sent back to Earth to seek out ones like themselves and spread the hunger for power and domination, until their numbers had grown so great that he, Roman, could see the proverbial light at the end of the tunnel.

Mankind had become so diseased that the Dark could almost sit back and watch the humans self-destruct. But Roman had never been one to sit by and let things unfold. He was an instigator and it gave him great pleasure to be the cause of chaos and hate.

Today was a bit of a special day for him because a small bit of Darkness had attached itself to the Guardian Ashton as she attempted to burn it from inside the mortal body of Wyatt.

It wasn't a lot, but just enough to give her a taste of the bitterness that selfless acts could leave behind. Roman knew she or her mate Sam would detect it soon enough and extinguish it. But for just a few hours it would be a thorn in her side and any little jab he could deliver to his foes was just plain old icing on the cake. Yummy!!

Roman rubbed his stick-like hands together in malicious glee and, as much as he would have loved to spy on the one infected, he had not the time. There was much he had to oversee and no time to waste.

Huffing out a sigh that reeked of rot, he squirmed his way across his domain and prepared to do what he did best.

Become a sower of seeds. The seeds of Darkness!

He laughed and gurgled all the way out his door, until only a trace of his mirth echoed in the dark.

This was a bonus not many alive or dead could claim, but he could. He could indeed! He got the pleasure of claiming he loved his job! And he got to claim that he was good at it. In fact he was the best!

The best at bringing horror and pain! When all was said and done, he was the one standing center stage to collect the big prize.

The ultimate prize.

The prize of souls.

Chapter 33

Haven woke while the shadows, her friends, were still pitch black and lay thick in the corners and draped like a heavy blanket over all they could reach.

The dim light of a new day was just beginning to chase her fellow Minions back into hiding when she opened her eyes and winced, as she tried to adjust to the glare of the suns rays. Tiny fingers of light fell across the dirty pillow where she rested her human head, making her groan and, like any other teenager, roll over and try to squeeze in just five more minutes of sleep.

After tossing and turning for those stolen few minutes she finally gave up and rose for the day.

Making her way into the filthy bathroom, she conjured some water and washed the sweat from her skin, trying to decide what to wear for the day.

Her normal black was chosen, but instead of the black lips and pale skin she was becoming known for, she added a light pink to her cheeks and a blood red stain to her lips. It never occurred to her that this deviation from her norm was anything to worry about. But the single spark of goodness that Hannah had found was growing and making its presence felt.

Still, weak as it was, the most it could influence was tiny things, hardly noticeable things. But still it was something.

No alarms were raised and Haven left her hovel and prepared to head into town and school.

Climbing into her car, she fired up the beast and sighed with the feeling of rightness that came with the deep purr of the engine. Slipping on a pair of dark sunglasses and turning on the radio was all she needed before pointing the nose of the car towards town and, giving it some gas, drove off in a cloud of dust.

The open window allowed the crisp morning air to fluff her dark mane, and it wasn't long before she began to hum along with her radio. Not the crap that they called music nowadays, but to music that had a good beat and drums that echoed in her chest. Yup, give her some hair band music and she was ready to roll.

She had just shut her car down when the door opened and a hand appeared to help her out. She knew that hand and she took it, rising up until she stood in front of the person it was attached to.

Wyatt looked good enough to eat as he refused to move away, giving Haven little room to stand without touching his body. So she did.

Dropping the helping hand, she raised one of her own until it rested on the wide chest that filled her vision, blocking out everything else.

The morning was cool and she could feel the heat the human radiated. She was drawn to it.

Keeping Wyatt at bay had accomplished everything she had hoped for. She could feel the need and want he harbored for her and she decided today was the day she would let down the walls she had erected.

"Well, well, well," she purred, as she dropped her eyes to follow her hand as it made a slow decent from the wide chest to the tight abdomen, not stopping until she went as far as Wyatt's belt would allow.

The rasping sound her nails made had Wyatt's muscles quivering. Her touch burned into him until he swallowed hard, wanting nothing more than her. Right now! Here! Spying eyes be damned!

"If it isn't the man of my dreams," Haven said, laughing inside at her choice of words. "What can I do for you?" she asked, again thinking her words clever.

"How about having lunch with me today?" Wyatt asked, his mind on fire with images from his dreams.

"Done!" Haven answered quickly, stepping to the side and closing her car door with a soft click, before bumping it with her butt to latch it all the way.

Wyatt noticed the move, as she intended, and felt his stomach jump with need.

Before any more could be said, they were joined by Wyatt's friends and, as a group, moved into the school to begin the day of learning.

Wyatt fidgeted through his classes and watched the clock until the bell rang, signaling lunch time. He dumped his books in his locker before making a bee line to the lunch room.

Walking through the line, he filled his plate with anything. He didn't care about the food. He didn't give it a second thought, before grabbing a seat and watching for Haven to come through the line.

It seemed like time crawled before she appeared with her tray and walked slowly to where Wyatt sat waiting.

"This seat taken?" Haven asked with a smile and dropped her food on the table beside his.

Wyatt cocked an eyebrow for an answer and waited for her to sit down before sliding just a little bit closer to her, letting their thighs touch, before he picked up his fork to eat.

Wyatt barely tasted his food as he watched in fascination as Haven mowed through hers like she was starving and this was going to be her last meal.

Rather than be disgusted at the crumbs that landed on her chest or the food that stuck to her mouth and chin, Wyatt wanted to bury his face in those breasts and Hoover up every last bit. He wanted to take his tongue and lick the drips off her chin and suck the chunks from the corners of her mouth.

He was on fire!

And Haven knew it.

Chapter 34

Wyatt was right about one thing, Haven ate with gusto. She wanted to make every bite count, for when she returned to her Dark form she would not eat again, and food just tasted so damn good, she couldn't help herself.

She watched as Wyatt took fewer and fewer bites until he stopped eating all together and just stared at her chest.

Haven crept into his mind and saw exactly what he was thinking and she made sure to dribble just a little more with her last bite, before smacking her lips in satisfaction and giving a huge sigh right after.

Taking both of her hands, she wiped slowly at the speckles on her breasts until they fell to her lap. Then she flapped her skirt until they fell to the floor, but gave her short skirt a few more flips, letting Wyatt imagine she was in need of a cooling breeze to kill the heat that collected there.

Taking the poor excuse of a napkin the school offered, she wiped at the food on her chin and lips, letting her tongue dart out and catch the chunks before they could fall or be collected.

Last but not least, staring straight into Wyatt's eyes, she licked each finger clean, sucking them one by one into her mouth until she was sure the human sitting beside her knew what she wanted. Until she was sure he wanted it too.

Hearing the bell ring, Haven piled her silverware on her tray and stood up.

"Got to go," she said, intending to make a hip swinging exit, but Wyatt stopped her with a hand on her arm.

"Hey," he began "how about after the game tonight we go out and grab something to eat?" Though it was posed as a question, Wyatt had no intention of letting her say no.

Haven considered saying just that, but decided now was as good a time as any to launch her physical attack on her victim. So instead, she shrugged her shoulders, as if it made no difference to her and said what he wanted to hear.

"Sure, why not." she purred in a husky, sexy voice.

Wyatt sat back down as Haven turned and walked away, swinging her hips with every step to seal the deal. His heart beat hard in his chest and his legs felt weak as he counted her acceptance as a victory.

Now all he had to do was get through the afternoon and the game before he was finally going to get to be with her alone.

He held his frustrations in until, by the time he was suited up and the whistle blew for the game to begin, he was feeling mean and itching to fight.

His muscles bunched and he mowed through the other team's line, seeing nothing but red. Only satisfied when his target lay beneath his body, gasping for the breath his hit had stolen from it.

Wyatt didn't offer a hand to the other player, only stood for a second, sneering down into the dazed, young eyes that stared back at him.

He trotted back to the huddle to accept the claps of appreciation on his back and listened to the cheers of the crowd as they applauded his abilities.

By the time the game was over the other team was grass stained and dirty, having paid a high price for being unlucky enough to be on the receiving end of Wyatt's frustration.

The team celebrated, the crowd cheered and Wyatt hunted for the one he could almost smell in their midst. Haven.

His eyes finally found her standing in the shadows of the bleachers, apart from the others and he liked what he saw.

Dressed in her usual black, she blended in with the night, making Wyatt blink to keep her in focus.

He licked his lips and wiped the sweat from his face as he took in her beauty and felt a rush, as he knew in his heart both of them were made for the Dark. Made for each other.

Leaving the field, he made his way to her side and, without a second thought, crushed her body against his and let his lips find hers.

He drank from her, as if in desperation, and tasted the Dark in her kiss. It tasted good, more than good, it tasted like life to him. A life he craved, with her.

Haven allowed the kiss and she opened herself to his hunger, allowing him to feed from her pool of blackness.

The pads he still wore bit into her flesh and she relished in the pain she could feel as a human. The sweet pinch of it, and the hunger for more, made her wrap her arms around him and pull him closer, until she could feel his desire for her. She wanted more. But not here. Not where eyes watched and tongues wagged.

She needed the darkness to do with him what she wanted, so she pulled back until his lips finally broke from hers.

"Go change," she whispered teasingly in his ear. "But hurry."

Wyatt did not have to be told twice and almost ran for the showers.

Ethan, watching the exchange of hungry affection between Wyatt and Haven, was once again forgotten

Chapter 35

Ethan had begun as everyone else in the stands had, cheering and rooting on his son's team. But by the end of the game he alone was silent. He alone found cause for concern.

Wyatt had always been good in sports and Ethan, as his father, had taken pride in the abilities that made his son shine in his games. Tonight was different. Tonight Wyatt had played to hurt, not to just win, and Ethan was scared.

Ethan watched his son bloody the other team and jerked every time the crack of Wyatt's tackles rolled like thunder off the field.

Ethan's worried eyes traveled the stands and he wondered why the other spectators did not see the madness that rolled off his son in waves. Was it his imagination he wondered? Was it because he knew Wyatt better than the others did or was it just his parental ESP kicking in to alert him to trouble?

Whatever it was, Ethan was glad when the game was over and Wyatt was off the field.

Standing up, Ethan made his way to the sidelines and intended to break tradition by going out on to the field to see his son. But he never got that far.

He watched as Wyatt almost ran into the shadows and, blinking his eyes, he finally saw what drew his son away.

Again it was the girl! The girl he had seen in the hallway outside the principal's office. The girl that seemed to always be in the dark.

Ethan watched as the two came together in a kiss that left him feeling like a peeping tom at a bedroom window.

When had his son grown up to be a man with feelings of passion, he wondered? Had he been that young, seventeen, when he began to feel such things? Looking back, he guessed he was, but it just seemed too young for his son. He was not ready to lose his boy to manhood.

Ethan was yanked back to the present when the two broke apart and Wyatt headed into the locker room.

Ethan watched the girl fade back into the shadows and, setting his shoulders, he went to stand at the doorway, meaning to catch Wyatt before he could take off.

He didn't have long to wait, as Wyatt walked out with his gear in a pack over his shoulder and a cloud of cologne surrounding him

Taking a deep breath, Ethan tried for casual as he blocked his son's retreat.

"Hey buddy," he started, getting his son's attention. "Want to go get something to eat?" Ethan asked, laying a hand on his son's shoulder in fatherly familiarity.

Wyatt looked at his father and felt a tug of irritation at the interruption to his plans.

"Hey Dad," Wyatt said, looking past him to where he had left Haven. "I can't. I've got a date."

"A date?" Ethan parroted. "With who, anyone I know?"

"Nope," Wyatt said, trying to step around his father.

"Well, who is she?" Ethan asked, matching Wyatt move for move so he was forced to stop and talk.

"Just a new girl in school," Wyatt said, looking over his dad's shoulder since he obviously was not getting past.

"What's her name? Who are her parents? Where does she live?" Ethan rapidly fired questions at his impatient son.

Wyatt's eyes became hooded and he dropped his pack between them with an angry thud.

"Look Dad," he began, his tone giving his dad the brush off. "We can talk tomorrow, okay? Right now I have to go."

"No, I don't think it is okay," Ethan said, keeping a wary eye on the man child before him. Ethan knew his son and the body language he was picking up was anything but friendly.

"You haven't really talked to me for a few weeks now and I think you can take a few minutes right now to fill me in. Or the only place you will be going tonight is home with me." Ethan finished, not wanting to use this tactic, but Wyatt left him no other choice.

Wyatt considered, for a moment, just shoving his old man down and stepping over him to find Haven. But before he could act on the impulse, his anger seemed to vanish.

Ashton stood behind him, with hands of fire, buried in his back. She gritted her teeth as she squeezed hands full of the Dark inside Wyatt until the muck turned to ash. As it did, the anger the boy felt seemed to die down and he was shocked that he could have harbored such feelings for his father, strange feelings of rage and not caring if he hurt his father emotionally or physically. He felt sick.

"Sorry Dad," Wyatt said, hanging his head and drooping his shoulders. "Her name is Haven and she just started a few weeks ago. I don't know her parents or where she lives either," Wyatt admitted.

"The best I can do is take you over to meet her and introduce you to her," Wyatt offered, extending an olive branch between them.

Ethan relaxed and breathed easier as it seemed his son came back to him.

"Deal!" Ethan said, reaching down to lift the gear from the ground and turned to walk beside Wyatt into the shadows.

Ashton stayed where she was, breathing hard in anger. The Dark she had rid Wyatt of had been strong. Strong and aggressive, not like the little dab of crap that Sam had pulled from her yesterday.

She had been totally unaware that a small bit of Wyatt's Darkness had gotten a hold of her, until Sam had plunged a hand into her belly and come out with a squirming spot of ooze.

She had wanted to throw up with disgust, but Guardians did not show such weakness. So instead, she had told Sam to drop the thing. It tried to get to a shadow to hide, but Ashton had ground it to nothing under her heel and kept grinding until it was no more.

She had underestimated the power of what Wyatt harbored, but she would not make that mistake again.

Tonight she too had watched from the side lines as Wyatt played, waiting until she had an opportunity to work her magic. She had almost waited too long before acting. But she had calmed Wyatt and Sam had worked on Ethan until father and son were once again as they should be.

"Let's get out of here," Sam said. "I don't want Haven to find us just yet."

Ashton agreed and both took off, leaving the humans to walk away as friends once more.

Once the mortals slept, the Guardians would be back, back to continue the fight for not one soul but two.

The outcome still uncertain.

Chapter 36

Haven watched from the shadows as Wyatt's father passed her to stand by the school's door, waiting for Wyatt, she was sure.

She stepped back until the shadows cloaked her body and was witness to the exchange between the two mortals. A smile had bloomed on her face as she anticipated a bit of a fight as Ethan tried to delay their date. She was sure her hold on Wyatt would not allow any hesitation. She was wrong.

She could not hear what was said, but the body language she observed told the story just as well.

She smiled and gloated as Wyatt clenched his fists and dropped his bag, almost in a challenge before his father's feet.

But her glee did not last, as she watched Wyatt's shoulders sag and his head bow to his father.

Her lip curled when Ethan picked up Wyatt's gear and both started walking towards her. She was so intent on watching father and son that she missed the faint glow that would have alerted her to the fact that a Guardian was on hand. But that information flew right over her head to disappear along with Ashton and Sam.

Haven watched the two as they approached her, noticing how they smiled and were at ease with each other. She could feel the love they both had for each other and her stomach rolled, wanting to disgorge the hot dog and nachos she had wolfed down during the game. Throwing up was not on her top ten things she liked to do, so she gritted her teeth and swallowed the bitter mass until she got control, just in time to face her enemy.

She knew Ethan was her enemy. She could smell the goodness he carried from a mile away. She could see it in his eyes, the compassion he had, the love he held, and the drive he accepted to help any who had less than his family.

He was one of the good ones and she wanted to step back as they stopped before her. But she didn't.

Taking her eyes off Wyatt, she locked gazes with Ethan and she knew the second he found out about her.

Ethan drew in a sharp breath as he stared into pools of blackness, seeing what his son did not. He had always heard that the eyes were the windows to the soul and he was now faced with proof that this old wives' tale was grounded in truth.

Instead of seeing the beautiful dark eyes that haunted Wyatt's dreams, Ethan saw the flat black orbs that carried the torments of Hell.

Ethan saw the flawless face melt and run until it looked like nothing he had ever seen before.

He saw the mouth turn into a black hole with long sharp teeth jagged and crusted with filth.

He saw the black snake like tongue slither out and drop dark drool onto its chin and the ground, turning the living grass into clumps of death.

He saw her true self that no human was supposed to see.

He saw danger to his son and he knew he could not stand by and allow her to take Wyatt from him.

In the silence of the moment Ethan saw all.

He saw his own death.

Chapter 37

Wyatt was oblivious to the under currents between Haven and his father as he made the introductions.

"Dad I'd like you to meet Haven and Haven this is my father, Ethan Goodwin." he said, standing to the side as the two, instant adversaries, faced each other.

"So you're Wyatt's daddy," she said, making her voice drip honey while she extended her hand for the acceptable shake. "Nice to meet you."

Ethan looked at the small, pale hand offered to him and wanted to hide his own deep in his pockets to avoid touching it.

"Don't touch it!" the thought screamed in his mind over and over. But with Wyatt watching, he had no choice unless he was prepared to explain why.

Reaching out with his hand, Ethan clasped Haven's. He felt a coldness whip up his arm and wanted to cry out at the pain it caused. But he didn't.

Gritting his teeth and pasting on a fake smile that didn't come close to reaching his eyes, Ethan fought back the only way he could think of. His grip, that started out weak and hesitant, turned into raw power as he squeezed until his muscles stood out in his arm.

Years of hard work on the ranch had made his muscles hard, and he used every bit of his strength now, not caring if she whimpered in pain, because he knew deep down she would not.

And she didn't.

Haven took everything Ethan could give her and smiled right to his face, letting him know he didn't stand a chance against her. She was more than mortal. She was the Dark. She was his worst nightmare!

Ethan dropped her hand and stepped closer to his son, wondering what to do.

"Tell you what," Ethan began, speaking to both teenagers, but keeping his eyes on Haven. "I was just asking Wyatt if he wanted to grab a bite to eat. How about I buy both of you something?" he said, stalling for time until he could come up with a reason to nix this date.

Wyatt opened his mouth to decline but Haven beat him to it, speaking first.

"Sure," she said, her eyelids lowering over pools of hate, "why not."

Wyatt rolled his eyes and groaned out his embarrassment as his father had just insinuated himself in the date that he had been craving.

"Good," Ethan said, stepping back and turning to go. "Why don't we just take my truck to the new hamburger place and then I can bring you back when we're done?'

"That's okay," Haven said, reaching out with the hand that Ethan had tried to break, linking her fingers with Wyatt's. "We can take my car and just follow you," she said, smiling up into human eyes that looked down at her. Wyatt's fingers closed on hers, letting her know he approved of her idea.

Unless he wanted to make a scene, Ethan had no choice but to shrug his shoulders and agree before heading to the parking lot with the two teens following behind.

"Follow me," he reiterated, before sliding into his truck and starting it up. He waited and watched until a sleek black muscle car's lights came on and the engine purred to life.

Taking the lead, Ethan made quick work of the drive to the burger place and all three walked in, found a seat and their orders were taken right away.

Haven was actually on her best behavior during the meal, answering all of Ethan's questions with memories of her human life.

There was no dropping of crumbs on her chest as she ate this time, but there was twining of feet under the table and brushing of thighs to make sure Wyatt kept his mind on her and not on his father.

Ethan drug out the meal for as long as he could, eating dessert he didn't want and having coffee to linger over. Having run out of excuses to fall back on, he was forced to bid the two eager teens good night and take his leave after telling Wyatt to be home by midnight.

Rolling his eyes, Wyatt agreed just to get him gone and have Haven to himself.

He stood in silence as he watched his dad drive away, waiting until his tail lights winked out before turning to the patient Haven and leading her back to her car. He helped her in, much to her amusement, before sprinting around the hood and folding his long frame into the passenger seat.

Wyatt ran his finger up and down her thigh as she drove them back to the school and his truck, before shutting everything off. Only the faint ticking of the motor cooling broke the silence until Haven turned in her seat to face him.

A hunger grew in Wyatt until he reached out and pulled her to him, making the gear shift dig into her hip, only letting up when she sat on his lap and her lips were within his reach.

Once again he tasted the Dark on her lips. Its bitterness tasted like sweet nectar on his tongue. He sucked it deep into himself, drinking it in as if he would die without it, only stopping when she allowed him to move his mouth to her neck and lower.

His hands filled themselves with her flesh, not satisfied until he had moved her shirt aside and freed her breasts to the cool night air and his hot moist tongue.

Haven let her head fall back as the human sensations rolled like waves through her body. When she had been alive she had had a handful of experiences, but nothing like this and she wallowed in the deliciousness of it.

Something inside her fought to let her forget her purpose, but in the end the feelings of Darkness overcame and she growled deep in her throat as she became the aggressor.

She bit at human flesh as each article of clothing was torn from Wyatt's body, nips at first until their combined clothes flew with a frenzy of hot desire and a need for instant gratification.

The bites her sharp teeth now took went deep and she licked the blood that ran from her marks before reaching down and laying the seat almost flat. Swinging her leg over him she lowered herself until she could rub her wetness up and down his length over and over until he was almost to the breaking point.

She stopped long enough to allow his seeking mouth to fill itself with her breast and his belly with her blackness, before reaching down a hand to feel the wetness she had left in his lap.

Her nails grew long and she scratched them up and down his length, until he bit down hard on the nipple he suckled in his mouth.

He was beyond knowing that the screams and cries he heard were not of this world.

All he could hear were the lyrics *"I'm on the highway to hell"* as he entered her body and sealed his fate.

Without a second thought he hit the gas.

Chapter 38

Ethan pulled into his yard and, against his better judgment, turned off his truck. He wanted to go find his son and drag him home where he could keep an eye on him. But the time for thinking of his boy as just that, a boy, was at an end.

He let his eyes look around the yard and thoughts of Wyatt were forgotten. Something was off, but what was it, he wondered?

He sat still for a moment before getting out and walking to the door. He went in and shut it with a click behind him, still no closer to finding out what nagged at him.

Sam was waiting for him when he shut the door and he knew Ethan's troubles.

"Come and sit," he whispered to him, guiding Ethan to do his bidding.

As Ethan sat with a frown on his face, Sam laid his hands on the tense shoulders and pulled the worries from his mortal mind, until the man could climb the stairs and get the rest he needed.

Sam stayed, intending to be there when Wyatt came home and add support while Ashton worked on him, but his plans were derailed as he heard a soft mew of distress coming from outside.

Wings opened wide, as he prepared to see what was wrong, but that was as far as he got before the air trembled with the roar of a lion and he heard a call for Saul spew out.

"Saul!" Callie mewed in sadness. "Saul!" she roared again, not calling this time but demanding.

Saul and Sam arrived at the same time, each ready to do battle at the call from the small Guardian.

Callie did not spare a glance at Sam, as she bounded to Saul, skidding to a stop at his feet.

"Hurry!" she said, turning to lead the way without explanations.

They did not have to go far before the reason for the cry for help was revealed to them. Sam was right, he was not needed. This was for Saul. Stepping back, he let the two be, staying close in case he was needed, but not interfering.

"Do something!" Callie wailed, standing over the mortal protector that struggled to breath.

Saul knelt down and laid his hands on the massive body, taking the pain he felt into himself, until the protector rested easier.

"Do something!" Callie demanded. "You've done it before. Do it again!"

Saul looked, with sad eyes, at Callie and he knew the feelings of loss she was fighting.

It was true that he had extended Gabriel's life well beyond what was normal to allow him to be on hand to protect the humans he loved. But this time he could not. He ached with that knowledge.

"Not this time," he said softly to Callie, as he stroked the dying animal's big head. "It's time for him to go," Saul said, looking into the big brown eyes that carried so much love for the human race.

Callie roared out her denial and the ground shook with her rage. Her teeth grew long and her claws deadly, as she prepared to fight for the life of her true friend she had become attached to.

Gabriel gave one last sigh before his spirit left his mortal body and stood before Saul and Callie, strong and massive once again.

"Hello Callie," he whispered, testing out his new voice. "I have waited a long time to meet you." he said, lowering his head to bring their noses together in friendship.

"I always knew there was someone by my side helping me, but I could never see you. I just felt you." he said quietly, trying to comfort her.

Callie's small body trembled, her face wet with the tears her beautiful eyes cried.

"I'm sorry." she mewed "I didn't want your life to end. I'm so sorry I couldn't do more. To give you a longer life with those you loved." she sobbed.

"Do not cry for me little one." Gabriel said, licking each of her tears away with a gentle tongue. "I will be waiting for my human friends when their time comes to join us. So you have nothing to be sorry for. I have had a rich life here on Earth and it has truly been one filled with love and goodness. I am okay with my fate and I thank you for watching over me as well."

Callie buried her tiny face in the forever soft fur, taking in his words. But still her heart broke with the loss of her charge and friend.

Saul gave them their time alone, but had to step in as the time for Gabriel to take his next step grew close.

Saul raised his face to the night sky and sent out a call for the leader of all animals to come to him. He waited. But not long.

Saul's eyes scanned the horizon until he spied a whirlwind in the distance. He watched until it grew huge in size and came straight for him and the others.

When it drew close enough for them to see, the base was not wind at all, but the coming of Omega, the Immortal Leader of every animal that walked the Earth.

When the beast came to a stop before Saul, the wind died down and the dust settled. The bright moon light revealed an Immortal that caused awe in some, fear in others and terror for those that foolishly crossed him.

"I have come," a deep voice said. "What do you need?"

Saul nodded his head in acknowledgement before stating his cause. "We need your help" he said to the fearless one before him, and much to Sam's amusement Omega answered.

"Speak!"

Chapter 39

Sam had never met Omega before, only having to deal with Immortal Guardians like himself, but he had to admit that the beast talking with Saul was beyond impressive.

Omega stood on all fours, but was as tall as the Guardians before him. His coloring was that of a wolf, only richer in the blacks, grays and silvers that covered his muscled body. The wings that lay upon his back were not made of sturdy feathers but instead were long, flowing hair the same color as his pelt and seemed almost alive as the strands moved with the breeze that blew softly, no longer the whirlwind of power Omega traveled with.

His large eyes were of molten silver and showed the strength and wisdom of his true being. He was the fierce protector of animals and the bringer of retribution for any and all who would abuse those animals. He was known to some as Karma.

The teeth, that grew long and sharp from his mouth, bit deep and carried pain to the humans the Dark used to torture the innocent souls of his charges. He made sure that when it was time for retribution no mercy was given.

As Sam stood and watched, the wind once again picked up until it shrieked and howled as if in agony.

Sam's hair swirled around his head and his eyes sought out the gales source until he noticed dust was once again coming their way. He watched as Saul and Omega grew silent, each turning into that wind, waiting for what was to come.

And what came, once again, left Sam in awe.

For a second time a beast emerged from the cloud of dust and came to stand at Omega's side. But this one was different.

Where Omega was powerful and fierce this one, his mate, was pure beauty.

Her coat was the color of the palest dawn and her wings were soft and lush as they brushed the ground behind her.

"I heard the call," she said, her voice musical and hushed. Turning to Saul, she whispered, "What can we do?"

"Hello Alpha," Saul said, greeting her as an old friend. "This is Sam," Saul supplied before he went further. "Sam this is Alpha, the mother of all earthly animals."

Her soft brown eyes swung to meet Sam's and he bowed his head in acknowledgement.

"Hello Sam," Alpha said, approaching him to catch his scent and judge his goodness. Satisfied, she returned to her mate's side and settled to listen to why Saul had called Omega to him.

Sam knew the story of the two Great Spirit wolves, as did every other Immortal, but he had never had the chance to meet the pair in person.

As he looked at the two standing side by side, the tale refreshed its self in his head and in his heart.

The soft and beautiful Alpha was the beginning of all animals, the Mother.

As each newborn came into the world she greeted them with a gift. The gift of a heart so large it could carry love, not only for its kind, but for the humans each one claimed as its own.

She empowered them with the gift of empathy too, so each could be a beloved member of a human family, give comfort when needed, but also to know the joys of a soft hand and a full belly.

But her work, and those that were chosen as animal Guardians, was never ending for, try as they might, the Dark found a way to enter some of the mortals and when that happened the animals suffered.

Small bodies were helpless to ward off hands and feet that hurt them, until a kind hearted human was found to rescue them or until their pain ended in death. When that happened Alpha became vengeance.

Her howl for her mate would ring out, as ugly as she was beautiful, until Omega came to her side. Together they made the bringer of pain pay until blood ran deep and they felt what it was like to endure pain and suffering from those greater than they.

Alpha may have been the beginning, the starter of it all, but Omega was the end. He was the punisher!

He made sure justice was exacted for each innocent life taken too soon.

They were a pair, these two Immortal beasts, Alpha and Omega.

The beginning and the end!

And Saul needed their help.

Chapter 40

As Alpha stood by her mate, her soft brown eyes fell on the spirit of the St. Bernard standing over its mortal body, looking scared and confused.

"Hello Gabriel," she said "My name is Alpha. I have come to give you a choice."

Gabriel turned his scared brown eyes up until they were captured and held by the female Guardian before him.

"Callie," he said, inching closer towards his friend and protector.

"It's okay Gabriel," she said, drying her tear drenched eyes with her paw. "This is Alpha. She's the first female of our kind." Callie supplied. "You can trust her."

Alpha moved closer until she was able to rub her face in the soft fur and give the silky fur a lick with her tongue.

Gabriel's fears seemed to die down until he sat back on his haunches and cocked his head.

"What choice?" he asked, no longer afraid.

"You now have the choice of becoming a Guardian like Callie," Alpha explained "Or you can move on and join your friends who are waiting for you."

As Alpha spoke a beautiful moonbow reached down from the sky and stopped before the big dog's paws.

Gabriel cocked his head and listened. He could hear faint echos of voices barking and rumbles of purring coming from above. Looking up, he saw friends that had passed through his life, wagging their tails and mewing in greeting.

"What is this?" Gabriel asked, not believing his eyes.

"You know what this is." Alpha said, making him admit what he saw.

"But I thought they were all dead." Gabriel said.

"They are," Alpha agreed. "And so are you," she finished, helping him accept his fate.

"You may join them or, as I said, you may choose to be a Guardian and stay here." Alpha continued, having all the time in the world to spend with this spirit.

"Are they okay?" Gabriel asked, having recognized a few that he knew had been sick or injured when they had come into his life.

"They are happy, healthy, warm and loved," Alpha assured him. "There is no pain here, no hunger, no sadness, nor anything to hurt them. There is only happiness and love. Would you like to join them?" she finished, wanting him to make the choice that would decide where he went from here.

"I can't stay here? With my humans?" he asked, even though he knew the answer already. He could read the answer in the soft brown eyes of the she wolf.

"But who will watch over them and keep them safe if I'm not here?" he asked, still caring what happened to his family.

"That's why I've called you here," Saul stepped in, looking at Omega.

Bright silver swung until eyes met and Omega waited.

"The Guardians, I, need a replacement for Gabriel," Saul began, only to be interrupted by Omega.

"Why?" the great wolf asked.

All fell silent as Saul told the tale of Leonard and now Wyatt. He told them of the need to keep this soul safe and fight the Dark that came to claim it.

Again Omega asked, "Why?"

Sam leaned a little closer, as it appeared Omega was going to force Saul into admitting why Leonard's soul was so important to him. He too was curious.

Saul's shoulders became tense and his mouth thinned as he tried to keep the information to himself, but in the end he had no choice. He needed help and he was not going to get it unless he came clean and satisfied the curiosity surrounding him.

"Because I failed," he finally said. His tense body relaxing as the weight of the secret was taken from his shoulders at last.

"Go on," Omega said, sitting on his haunches, getting comfortable.

"When Leonard came to us he was very young," Saul said, telling his tale. "He was too young to be given the responsibility of being an Immortal Guardian."

"Younger than him have been given the powers of a Guardian," Omega cut in. "Why do you think he was too young, this Leonard?"

"He missed his human family too much," Saul admitted. "I thought if he could be among the humans he would get over this and move on. But he never really did. Instead, he wished for a playmate and ended Ashton's life before her time. He caused chaos and, in the end, Roman almost turned him."

"So, why did you not just send him on his way after the last time?" Omega questioned. "Why is he back and not moving on?"

"Because I was soft," Saul admitted, the taste of his choice was now like dirt in his mouth.

"Because of my choice, Leonard liked the power he received as a Guardian and no longer wanted to move on. Even when his family passed, he showed no interest in being with them anymore," Saul supplied.

"So this is the reason Roman still tries to capture this soul, correct?" Alpha asked.

"I believe so," Saul agreed. "I think Roman senses the hunger for power that this soul craves and he is using this to bring him to the Dark side."

"So you now fight for what exactly?" Omega asked, not seeing why the most powerful of all the Immortal Guardians did not just put an end to this losing battle.

"I fight to keep this soul for the side of good and to give it a chance to be reunited with its human family beyond the Great Gates," Saul admitted all.

"And?" Omega prompted.

"And to atone for my mistake in judgment," Saul finally said.

Saul waited as Alpha and Omega looked into each others eyes, communicating without words, until a decision had been reached.

"We will stand with you," Omega said, causing Saul to relax with relief. "We ask again, what do you need?"

"A warrior!" Saul said.

"I need a warrior!"

Chapter 41

The yips and mews from above that had quieted during Saul's story, now started again, reminding the wolves they had business to attend to themselves.

Turning once again to Gabriel, Alpha nudged his strong shoulder and asked, "Have you made your choice little one?"

Gabriel bowed his head. He had listened to the talk of protecting and guiding and he had felt a tug in that direction. But he was tired. So very tired and he wanted to be with the friends that had gone before him.

He wanted to run and play and be happy until the time came for his masters to join him. He wanted to be waiting for them as they crossed through the Great Gates so they had a friend to meet them with unbridled joy and happiness.

He missed Mattie and he knew she waited for him. He could see her smiling and calling to him as she had done so many times in life.

He chose.

"I choose to move on," the great dog said to Alpha. "As much as I would like to stay and protect the humans, I would like to rest more. I think I am finished here."

Nodding her head in understanding, the she-wolf stepped aside and the rainbow, that was so filmy before, became solid and real.

"We will see each other again," she assured the dog and, after one faltering step, Gabriel bounded up and up until his friends surrounded him in joy and happiness.

Mattie, too, joined in the celebration and stroked the head of the companion she had loved in life, and now in death.

"Welcome home Gabriel," she said lovingly, as the rainbow faded and took the celebration with it. The last the group of Guardians saw were tales wagging and bodies jumping in happiness and play. Friends parted had now become friends reunited again.

Alpha leaned into her mate and her heart shared its sorrow and gladness with his, until once again they stood as one before Saul.

"Tell us what we can do to help," Omega said, his mind once again on the business at hand.

"As I said before," Saul replied "I need a protector for the humans here. Ethan and Wyatt need to have a companion that will warn us of danger and keep watch until we arrive."

Omega's mind flew through the possibilities, trying to find one that would meet the demands as Saul had explained. He knew that whomever he picked would have to battle the Dark, and maybe even Roman, so the warrior Saul asked for had to be strong, fierce and brave.

Omega made his choice and stepped before the Immortal.

"I shall be your warrior," he said in his deep voice.

The deep growl that came from Alpha's throat made the ground shake and the trees rattle.

"There are others that can do this job," she barked angrily. "Why must it be you?"

Omega nuzzled his mate, as he rested his head along side hers.

"I know the dangers," he said softly, as his warm breeze of breath caressed her ear. "I think that if Roman really wants this soul, now might be the perfect time to catch him, while he is distracted, and put an end to him. We can't risk letting this opportunity pass us by. I must be here to make sure it does not!"

Alpha could not deny that Omega's plan had merit, but that did not mean she had to like it.

Bowing her head in acceptance, she licked his face once, in an expression of her love, before turning to walk to Saul.

Her beautiful pale hair stood on end and her muzzle curled in a threat. The teeth she bared grew long and sharp as daggers and her tongue crept out to feel their points. Soft brown eyes that held all the love in the world for her charges, grew hard and rimmed in red as her voice rumbled with thunder as she spoke.

"I will hold you responsible should anything happen to Omega," she growled out. "Even though we fight on the same side, the side of good, if anything happens to my mate, I will come for you and I will bring all of hell with me!"

Omega walked to her side and nipped at her neck to make her back down, but she would not. She turned those feral eyes upon him and he saw the truth of her words in them.

Omega opened his mouth to speak to Saul but the Guardian held up his hand to stall his words.

"You, my friend, are the luckiest of creatures. You have the eternal love of a mate, and a fierce one, that will battle for you and beside you. I envy you," Saul replied humbly, bowing his head.

Omega still did not like the threat that was issued by Alpha, but he was appeased as the mightiest of the Immortal Guardians smoothed the situation with his kind words of reassurance and understanding.

"How will you get the humans to accept me as a member of their family?" Omega wanted to know, changing the subject, bringing it back to the matter at hand.

"I will help with that," Sam said, stepping forward and drawing all eyes to him. "I will get Ethan to see the good in you and feel a need to keep you close since his friend has passed on. Ashton will do the same with Wyatt, although she may have a harder time since he carries the Dark inside him now."

"I just need to know when," Sam finished.

"Make it tomorrow morning," Saul said, and looked to Omega for his approval.

"Give them time to grieve their loss and bury Gabriel's body before you do." Alpha said. "You owe that to Gabriel."

"Of course," Omega said. "I will come here tomorrow night and by then you should have helped both to move on. But do not take the memories of Gabriel from them. He was important and should be remembered as such."

"Agreed," Sam and Saul said together.

"Thank you," Saul said. "I will see you tomorrow."

"Let's be off," Omega said to Alpha, as the wind that carried him picked up speed.

"Remember my words!" Alpha said, before turning to leave with her mate "Do not forget!"

"Not a chance," Sam whispered, as he watched the wind carry the two beasts away.

"Not a chance!"

Chapter 42

Sam stayed behind when the others left, keeping watch over the mortal remains of the loyal pet until head lights lit up the darkened yard.

Wyatt's truck pulled in and purred to a stop. The motor was shut off, leaving nothing to disturb the silence of the night once again.

Sam watched as the boy got out and slammed the door, not even trying to be quiet, before he started towards the front door.

Sam did not try to hide, as Wyatt could not see him, but he forgot the Dark inside the human, and he tensed when Wyatt hesitated and sniffed the air. The Dark inside him alerted him to danger and he searched with eyes of black until he zeroed in on the spot where the Guardian stood.

Sam still did not move, but waited to see what the mortal would do next. He expected him to come closer, but he did not. Instead, something else drew his attention and he moved away, with Sam following.

Sam heard the Dark whispers coming from the shadows as Wyatt approached the body Gabriel had left behind, until the Dark voices shrieked and moaned in united encouragement.

They giggled and chanted, telling the boy what to do and he listened.

Wyatt stuck out a foot and used his toe to nudge the lifeless body. After he was satisfied of its death, he reached into his pocket and pulled out a small lighter, flicking it to fiery life.

He held the flame up high until he could look upon his friend, standing still as a statue, listening to the voices in his head.

Sam expected him to turn and go back to the house, but Wyatt lowered the flame until it halted just inches from the furry, lifeless body.

Sam narrowed his eyes, preparing to leap forward should Wyatt try and touch the flame to Gabriel, but he was too slow.

Ashton stood behind the boy, with hands on fire and wings opened wide. She whispered to him in a voice filled with wrath.

"What you do to this body, I will do the same to you! Think carefully and choose wisely, because the price you will pay will be your life and you will know the pain of fire like no other!"

Sam watched as Ashton's lips curled and her flames danced higher, until her hands were inches from the boys back, and she had but to move a hair's breadth and he would become a living torch.

Ashton breathed out smoke and wanted nothing more than to dig her hands in deep until this pain in the ass teenage mortal felt himself burn. Burn like he was imagining the body of his lifetime pet was going to do when he dropped the lighter he held.

"Do it!" she taunted. "Do it and die!"

Her words must have reached him at last, for he took one step back and then another until he extinguished the light and walked back to his house.

Before going in though, he stopped and looked back over his shoulder in the direction of Sam and Ashton, letting his lips pull back until his teeth gleamed in the dark.

"Ain't no fun unless they're alive anyway!" Wyatt taunted, before ducking into the house and locking the door.

Ashton's chest rumbled with a growl of rage. But hers was not the only one as Omega, in the form of a mortal wolf, stepped from behind a tree and joined them.

"You saw?" Sam asked, when the rumbles of anger died down.

"I saw!" Omega snarled, licking the drool from his lips as he imagined the human's throat in his jaws.

"Tell me again why Saul wants this soul protected!" Omega demanded, not seeing the point of protecting one who would burn a loyal friend's body, even if its soul had moved on. And not just burned it to bury the remains. No! Burn it because the doer of the deed was evil and enjoyed causing pain.

"This human is filth!" Omega said, beginning to think his offer for help was a mistake.

"Agreed!" Ashton said angrily, looking to Sam for answers.

"We do this because Saul asked it of us. We do this because it is important to him," Sam said, closing the book on the discussion.

Ashton and Omega looked at each other, neither one saying a word but neither one changing their opinion of Wyatt either.

"I thought you were not coming until tomorrow night," Sam said, changing the subject to a safer one, he thought.

Omega turned his big head and stared without blinking into Sam's eyes.

"Alpha thought it would be a good idea to watch over the body until it was found and could be buried," he said, sitting back on his haunches. "Obviously she was right."

Ashton turned her eyes to the house and watched Wyatt's light go out for the night.

"It won't be long now," she said. "He'll be asleep soon and I can get to work when he is."

"I'll stay with Ashton," Sam told the wolf. "Once the sun has come up and the burial completed, I will guide Ethan into accepting you. Then it will be up to you to stand guard and call if you need us."

"I know my role." Omega said, rolling his eyes at the redundancy of Sam's instructions.

Sam and Ashton opened their wings and started for the house.

"Thank you again." Sam said one more time before they went inside.

"Again, you are welcome." Omega said.

"Watch your back," Ashton warned, before disappearing from the wolf's sight.

Omega growled deep in his chest one last time before melting back into the night.

"The boy better watch his!" he said, as he smelled the evil around this place.

"The boy better watch his!"

Chapter 43

Ethan woke with the first light and stretched under the covers. It was warm and toasty there and he wanted to stay where he was for a few more minutes. But the chores would not wait and he had hungry mouths to feed, so he flipped the covers back and started his day.

After his coffee was made and poured into a favorite mug, he dished up a big bowl of dog food and went outside to feed his buddy.

Standing on the back porch, Ethan called Gabriel and waited, expecting to hear the thumping of huge feet and the happy barking of greeting, but he heard neither. Only the happy tweeting of the bids as they too began a new day.

He called again, adding a sharp whistle this time, and still nothing.

He finally figured out what had bothered him the night before when he drove into the yard. No dog came to greet him.

"Aw damn!" he muttered to himself, getting a sick feeling deep in his belly.

Ethan set the dish on the steps and walked the yard until he came to the final resting place of his beloved pet.

Taking off his cap, he wiped at the tears that gathered in his eyes, and knelt down to stroke a hand over the cold body on the ground.

He stayed that way, talking to Gabriel one last time, saying his good-byes before rising to wake Wyatt and share the chore of burying their dog. His soul hurt and his gut was raw with his loss.

He walked with feet of lead to go wake his son and break the news to him, promising his friend he would be right back.

Ethan got Wyatt up and, ignored his grumbling that it was Saturday and he wanted to sleep in, he left the room with a final warning to be downstairs in five minutes.

When Wyatt entered the kitchen with a frown on his face Ethan broke the news to him of the death in the family. For Gabriel had been as much a part of their family as they were.

Due to the night's work Ashton had done, Wyatt was able to feel sorrow at the loss and complained no more as they set to work digging a hole, and with gentle hands laid Gabriel's lifeless body in it.

When the dirt was in place and a cross with a favorite toy marked the spot, Ethan stepped back and looked out over the vista of his land. But he didn't see it. All he focused on was a lone wolf sitting a few feet away looking at them with cold steel eyes.

"I'll get the gun," Wyatt said quietly, as he began to back slowly towards the house.

Sam laid his hands upon the father's shoulders and whispered into his ear, "This one is a friend. This one is to be taken in."

"No," Ethan told Wyatt, holding up a hand to stop his movements.

Wyatt stopped, but thought his father crazy for not shooting the predator while they had a chance.

Ashton came to Wyatt and did the same as Sam, but her results were not as satisfying as Sams. Wyatt resisted her whispers and imagined pulling the trigger and splattering its insides all over. He wanted to see the blood and he wanted to be the one to cause death.

Ashton let her hands turn to flames as she dug them into Wyatt, not letting go until his thoughts faded and he remembered them no more.

She flung the blackness from her and nodded to Sam and Omega that the path was clear for Omega to be taken in.

Omega stood on long legs and let his tail wag in greeting before slowly approaching the humans, stopping in front of Ethan and sitting back down.

Ethan reached out a hand and stroked the thick fur, feeling its softness before releasing a held breath in relief.

"He seems friendly enough," he said to his son, encouraging him to come closer and pet the animal.

Wyatt did, but Omega had to bite down hard on his instincts not to crush the bones in the hand that smelled so strongly of Darkness. This one was bad and he knew it. He knew it deep down and he was sure, once again, Saul would fail in saving this one.

But he liked Ethan. Ethan was good and he focused on that hand as it stroked his back and rubbed his sides. He knew he would stay and help, if for no other reason than to protect the father.

Protect him from the son.

Protect him from the Dark.

Protect him from what was to come.

Chapter 44

The three made their way back to the house and the bowl of food meant for the beloved dog was given to the wolf. Ethan stayed and watched as the wolf sniffed the food before taking first one bite and then more in quick succession, making the man wonder when the last time was he had eaten.

When the bowl was clean Omega approached his charge and sat at his feet, letting him reach out a hand and stroke him in friendship.

Not so for Wyatt. The boy had backed up to the door and stood stiff legged, on guard while the food was consumed. He did not see an animal in need of a home and love. Instead he saw a threat, not to Gabriel's memory, but to his place of power in the family.

Wyatt felt threatened by the love he could already see in his father's eyes for, in his hooded eyes, what was nothing more than a filthy beast.

The voices whispered to him that this was an enemy and he should kill it. And he wanted to.

"What should we name him?" Ethan asked, raising his eyes to his son, waiting for an answer.

"Whatever," came the short reply, followed by a shrug of his young shoulders.

Ethan wondered what had his son's shorts in a knot, but the cold nose that bumped his still hand drew his attention away and he smiled as the wolf seemed to want his touch.

"How about Floyd?" Ethan suggested, knowing that the name fit their new pet to a tee.

Wyatt again shrugged his shoulders in indifference before grunting and heading into the house.

Ethan didn't care if Wyatt liked it or not, for he did, and the wolf seemed to be happy with it too.

"I hope you decide to stick around from now on," Ethan said, before thumping the side of the big wolf one more time before heading inside himself.

Omega rose from his seated position as soon as the door was closed and stood on stiff legs, with his fur standing high on his back. The stench of the Dark was so thick he could almost taste it on the tongue that licked his curled lips.

Omega looked down at Callie as she came to stand before him.

"Can I stay?" she asked, having formed an attachment to these humans.

"Yes little one," the wolf said, calming himself until he could think clearly again. "You can help keep watch over the mortals and my back." he said, not trusting Wyatt to not try and do him harm.

"Thank you," Callie said, with her head bowed.

"Can I too call you Floyd?" she asked, a twinkle of humor in her feline eyes.

Omega had never had a human name before and, as he thought about it, he became pleased with the idea of being called Floyd by his new friends. Or at least friend.

"Yes," he said "you may, but don't tell Alpha."

Callie purred in pleasure before jumping up to sit upon his shoulder as she had done for Gabriel.

She felt raw power under her paws and she shivered with the knowledge that, should he unleash it, the one it was aimed at would suffer greatly.

Teeth, muscle and nails would be wicked weapons and Callie doubted any Dark creature could stand against them.

"Where do I rest?" he asked his companion, wondering if he would be expected to go back into the trees to find his bed.

"There," Callie pointed with a tipping of her nose towards a fine dog house that Gabriel had used when alive.

The Leader of Animals made his way to the door and, seeing no danger, walked inside. He sniffed the corners, making sure no threat lurked inside, before turning so his eyes could see outside and laying down to rest his great head on his paws.

He huffed out a breath and settled down to watch the house and its occupants.

His watch had begun and he would count on Callie to be his eyes when sleep took him over.

But his senses where sharp and none would pass that meant to cause harm. Even Wyatt, he vowed.

He would stand against him and the Dark should the need arise, and he knew it would.

It already had a toe hold and he knew it was only going to get worse

With his belly full, his new body wanted to rest. He let Callie know what was expected of her before letting his eyes drift close and his breathing slow.

Callie purred in his ear, easing his rest, but she kept her eyes wide open, ever alert for the Dark.

She was small but mighty and, should the enemy come to call, she would protect her charges with the spirit and will of a lion.

But for this moment, she was happy

Chapter 45

Haven woke from her sleep, stretching and loving the feel of human muscles as they quivered and rippled to life.

She finished stretching, but instead of feeling relaxed and content she felt off.

The black river of Darkness that ran through her and coated her being was quiet and still on this morning and she wondered at the change. A feeling of alarm began as a tickle, but within seconds became a full fledged tidal wave as it tried to tell her to be on her guard, but Dee and Hannah stood by to silence its cry for help.

Both had been hiding in the small light Haven had left burning until she had returned and crawled into the filthy rags she called a bed.

The Dark had whispered to Haven that they smelled Guardians near by, but the small flickering light of goodness in her heart had lulled her to sleep before they could fully alert her to danger.

Hannah and Dee wasted no time in getting down to work once her dark eyes had closed and her chest rose in slow deep breaths.

Hannah found her way to the small light of hope in Haven's heart, smiling as it danced and greeted her with gladness. She stroked the flame, feeding it from her spirit, until it grew stronger and bulged against the Dark mass that crowded around it.

The Guardian knew her job and worked throughout the night, destroying the Dark a handful at a time until finally, calling it a night, she stood back and looked at her handy work.

The heart that had been black with sludge now gleamed pink and new, giving the light of hope and goodness a bigger space to work from and grow.

Hannah was tired from her night's work of cleaning out the sewer and she waited in the dawn's new light for Dee to join her.

As Haven began to stir, Dee had finally joined Hannah standing by the window, each shaking their hands and ridding themselves of the Dark that clung to them.

"How was your night?" Hannah asked Dee after she was finished.

"Well it was different," Dee supplied, running her clean hands through her dark hair.

Hannah raised an eyebrow in question, letting Dee know she needed more information to satisfy her curiosity.

"I found some more memories of her life," Dee began, giving her wings room to stretch after being cramped during her night's work.

"And?" Hannah prompted, wanting more.

"There just isn't much to work with there," Dee said, her eyes going sad at the lack of goodness Haven had experienced in her short human life.

"Instead of bringing out the good I've had to get rid of the bad so what she does remember seems more meaningful and fills up more of her thoughts. I think this will make her more accepting of good times and good people," Dee finished with a shrug.

Hannah chewed on her lip as she thought about what Dee had said. She wondered how they were going to turn Haven if they could not make her see the goodness the world had to offer.

"Maybe we have to let her have new experiences that are good and she will be able to build on them," Hannah offered as an alternative.

"Well she had a doozie of one last night," Dee said, her cheeks turning pink with the memory she had seen.

"Wyatt?" Hannah guessed and watched Dee nod her head and roll her eyes.

"Don't tell me," she said, correctly guessing at the activities the two teens had engaged in.

"She's got her hooks in him pretty deep and he's eating the Dark up fast," Dee said, deeply concerned.

"We better have a talk with Ashton and Sam then," Hannah said, preparing to leave to find the pair.

Dee walked back to the bed and looked down at the mortal and knew their night's work had at least a small affect, as a healthy pink glow kissed the cheeks that had been so pale just the day before. But for how long, she wondered? And would their work be enough to dig out the rot before Roman figured out what they were doing?

Leaning down, the beautiful Guardian placed her lips beside Haven's ear and whispered into it.

"Today will be a good day," she said. "Today everything you see, hear and touch will bring good memories to mind. You will see and want that good. Hold on to it. Keep it in your heart."

Dee finished by brushing a hand over the cheek closest to her before standing up straight and leaving the room. She had done what she could and tonight would show her if what they worked for would stick.

If not, they would have to go to a plan B and she was not sure they had one.

Turning one of the Dark Ones was hard work and usually not worth the trouble, but Saul wanted this one, so they would try.

She, sadly, had a feeling they were going to fail.

Chapter 46

Wyatt stayed around the home place for most of the day, keeping his eyes on the wolf that his father seemed to have adopted. He didn't like the way the silver eyes followed him, and he was sure the mouth twisted in hate when their paths crossed, which seemed to be often.

He watched, with jealous eyes, as his father seemed to love his new pet, and Floyd followed him around like it was the most natural thing in the world to do. Like they had been best buds forever.

Even the neighbors that came into the yard, after a first hesitation, seemed to accept the animal as a friend and not a threat. Wyatt had been sure that there would be such an out cry of fear and demand for its termination that he had hoped the whole damn county would show up. Then he would get a chance to put holes in its hide. But no.

Floyd wove his magic around each soul he met, until everyone wanted one just like him for themselves. Wyatt was disgusted.

When Saturday night rolled around, he went up to his room and got ready to go out, determined to hook up with Haven again and finally have something to brighten his weekend with.

Ethan put a stop to that by putting his foot down and saying no to the idea.

They talked, well Ethan talked and Wyatt pouted until it came down to Ethan having to say, "No and that's final," before the house became quiet and the air chilly with hostility.

After a silent supper, Ethan put on a coat and went outside to stand on the steps and look up into the clear night sky.

He wondered which star he should talk to if he wanted to have Mattie hear him and maybe come and sit a spell with him.

It was not Mattie who came to share his night, but a wolf with a cold nose and a warm body.

Floyd sat beside the human and leaned against him to share his warmth and hear his words as he talked out loud.

"What am I going to do about Wyatt?" he asked the night sky, draping his arm over the muscled shoulders of his companion.

"He's changed so much in the last few weeks that I can't seem to get through to him anymore. He seems so distant and angry. Not like the son I know, but more like a stranger. What do I do, Mattie?" he asked, letting his shoulders slump and a lump form in his throat.

Omega lifted his head to the skies and his eyes glowed silver as he sent out his own message to those that listened.

"Sam!" he called out. "Sam you are needed!"

Within seconds the Guardian landed in the yard and came to stand before the pair on the steps.

"What is it?" Sam asked, talking to Omega alone.

"Your human is having a hard time and I think he needs a little help," the wolf said.

Sam sat on Ethan's other side and listened, as Omega had intended, until he knew the problem that was plaguing his mortal.

He placed his lips to Ethan's ear and whispered until the tenseness left his body and Ethan finally smiled.

"Thanks Mattie," the human said, mistakenly thinking his wife had heard his call and given him advice.

Ethan gave the wolf one last squeeze before thumping its side and going into the house for the night.

"What did you say?" Floyd wanted to know, his mouth grinning as he found it amusing Sam had been mistaken for the lost loved one.

Sam too smiled, but was in no way offended, as many, many times before this one his words had been attributed to one who had passed on.

"I just told him most teenagers were a pain in the ass. But if he just stuck to his guns and showed the boy love, then maybe everything would be okay. That's all," Sam replied with a softening smile.

The grin fell from Omega's face and his eyes glowed as he thought about the distrust and Darkness that he felt from the human boy.

"He's bad you know. The boy, Wyatt or Leonard or whatever you want to call him. He's bad," Omega voiced his concern to Sam.

Sam nodded his head in agreement and both were silent as they wondered what the future held in store.

"We're trying our best to turn it around," Sam finally said out loud. "It's just doubly hard when the Dark has such a strong hold over a human. I'm not sure we can pull it off. Ashton's working every night and each time it gets harder and harder as more of the Dark infection, if you will, latches on every day."

Omega knew what Sam meant as he had smelled the rot grow stronger as the day had progressed. By the time the sun had gone down, Wyatt had reeked of the Dark, and Omega wanted nothing more than to destroy this human and the Dark presence he sensed.

But he had not. For the friendship he shared with Saul, he had not.

Sam heaved a sigh and stood up to face the house.

"Ashton will be here shortly and once again we will destroy as much of the Dark as we can. Sleep well my friend," he said before he turned to enter the house. "Keep one eye open when you do."

"I have Callie," Omega said, as the small Guardian jumped up on his shoulders and settled in the thick fur.

"I am his eyes while his body sleeps," Callie said. "Nothing shall harm him while I am here."

Sam liked the way the small one so fiercely guarded her charges and he was satisfied with the arrangements.

"Just be careful," Sam said before fading away, leaving the two animals alone.

"That's the plan," Omega said.

"That's the plan!"

Chapter 47

Ashton met up with Sam and together they entered Wyatt's room, expecting to see the boy curled up under the covers fast asleep. But he wasn't.

The bed was mussed and the pillows were lumped, giving a vague outline of a body under them. But a closer look would have given the ruse away.

Wyatt was not there.

"Nasty little turn of events," Ashton said, crossing her arms over her chest in disgust.

"Should we wake Ethan and let him know what's going on?" Sam asked, his head cocked to one side in thought.

"Let's go see if we can find the little brat first!" Ashton said angrily, opening her wings in preparation.

"Not going to be too hard to figure out where he went," Sam voiced with disgust, following Ashton's lead with his own wings spreading out.

"Let's go find Hannah and Dee and see if Haven is in her bed," Ashton suggested before leaping into the air and pushing down hard with her wings to gain speed.

It took only seconds before Ashton and Sam joined Hannah and Dee standing outside the wreck of a house that Haven called home.

"Is she there?" Ashton asked, short and sweet.

"Nope!" Hannah said, her eyes of red glowing in frustration. "I take it Wyatt is gone too," she said, guessing why the two Guardians had shown up unexpectedly.

"Do we go find them or let it be?" Dee asked, opening her mind to see if she could find where the two teens were at.

"Let it be for tonight," Sam said. "Unless we plan on dousing them with cold water, I think they are going to do what they want tonight come hell or high water."

Ashton didn't like it. She knew better than any of them how fast the Dark was growing in Wyatt, and to skip a night of cleaning would give the Dark a grip on the boy she might not be able to break.

She looked with her Immortal eyes and everywhere she looked she saw the shadows crawling with creatures that came out when the sun went down. Tracking the Dark, when there was so much of it, was a futile effort at best. At worst, a fight was likely to erupt and they were out gunned when the night took over the Earth.

"Being teenagers, I'm pretty sure they will be sleeping late tomorrow after their activities tonight. So I vote that we wait until dawn and use that time to pick up where we left off," Sam advised, shrugging his shoulders in defeat.

Before any of the rest could answer, the air began to crackle and the ground shook under their feet.

Four sets of wings unfurled and backs were turned until a protective circle had been formed by the Immortals standing in Haven's yard.

Battle stances were assumed and each was ready for what was coming at them.

Hunter and Jaxon landed with a boom and, seeing their fellow Guardians ready to do battle, they too faced outward and drew their weapons in readiness.

"Really Jaxon," Hannah said, standing down and walking to her mate. "You could have told us you were coming instead of just showing up," she said, landing a punch to his muscled arm.

"Didn't think of it," Jaxon said, grabbing her to his side and giving her a squeeze. "What's up?" he asked, wondering why it appeared a meeting had been called.

Dee walked over to Hunter and slid into his arms, frowning at the black that still dripped from his razor sharp wings.

"Been busy?" she asked, knowing the residue that clung to his wings was the blood from Dark foes.

"Nothing out of the ordinary," Hunter said matter of factly. "Jaxon and I just thought we would check in on you girls and see how things were going. Seems we got here just in time to sit in. So, what's up?"

Ashton filled them in on the missing teens and their decision to give it a rest until the two snuck back into their beds.

"If Ethan finds out, Wyatt will have to wait until night time before he gets to rest," Hunter said smirking, as he remembered his father working his ass off when he had pulled a stunt like that.

"If we wait too long it will be too late!" Ashton said sternly, drawing the attention of all as the expressions of amusement and reminiscing fell from their faces.

"I think it's time we talked to Saul." Jaxon said out loud, what the others were thinking.

"I heard," Saul said, coming to land quietly among his friends.

"Hannah, Dee how goes it with Haven?" the Immortal Guardian asked, investigating before he made a decision.

"I think we are making some head way," Dee said, telling Saul what she found out as she worked on turning the Dark One.

"I also think that every time Wyatt feeds from her the Dark looses its hold on her a little more," Dee said, and Hannah shook her head in agreement.

"But every time he feeds, as you say, the Dark grows more powerful in Wyatt," Ashton injected. "I can't pull it from him any more. Every day more is left after I am finished until, like I said, it is going to be too late to save this soul."

"Tonight I will take your place" Saul said to Ashton. "Maybe I will have better luck in getting to the root of the evil planted in Wyatt's soul. Maybe not. We will meet here again tomorrow night and talk again."

With that, Saul spread his wings and left the group to stand looking after him until they could see him no more.

"One more night," Ashton conceded, as tiny flames began to lick at her fingers as anger grew in her. "I'll give it one more night and then we have to figure something else out or wash our hands of the whole deal. It may be time for the mortal to pass on and his soul to be taken."

"Taken by whom though?" Hunter questioned.

Ashton was silent.

She had no answers.

Chapter 48

Wyatt and Haven had indeed come together, but unlike his Guardian counter parts, Roman knew exactly where they were.

He knew because he stood in the deep, dark shadows of the night and watched as the two reached with hands of lust and joined when their bodies were on fire from wanting.

As clothes dropped to the ground, as teeth and claws came out, as souls were fed from the never ending river of Darkness, he watched.

Black drool ran from his lips and pooled at his feet as he watched the Dark pass from Haven to Wyatt and the boy ate it up and asked for more.

He watched as Wyatt's being turned dark as night and he smiled in satisfaction of a plan coming together.

Roman's smile did not last long, as he saw Haven empty herself of the Dark for Wyatt. Instead of filling back up, her mortal body stayed the color of smoke, grey and wispy.

Roman's satisfaction turned to anger! He knew what the Guardians had been up to. He knew they worked on taking his minion from him and hoping the lust Wyatt felt for her would pull him along in her wake.

"Did they think he was stupid," Roman wondered? "Did they really think they could hide their treachery from him?"

The night grew deep and dark around Roman as his anger grew at being duped, until the few leaves that clung to the dormant trees were whipped from their branches. Those same trees bent with the force of the cold wind of Roman's anger until they moaned in pain and cried, "No more!"

Omega stood still in the night, listening to the moans and shrieks that the foul wind carried and he knew trouble was afoot.

The Dark had come out to play, and not just any Dark he figured, but one of power from the way the cold wind had appeared and from the rotting stench that it carried on its gusts.

The mortal wolf lifted his nose to the sky and howled its warning for all to hear. Humans shivered at the loneliness the one long note carried, and those out in the night hurried for cover, lest they be caught in the jaws of the predator that was wandering and on the prowl.

But they had nothing to fear, as it was not food Omega hunted on this night. He hunted for the Dark One that had set the winds to howling and the trees to quaking. He hunted for the teens that hid from prying eyes. He hunted for Roman!

No sooner had the last of his cry faded into silence before the wind grew even more violent, as seven sets of Immortal wings beat the air into a frenzy, and seven Guardians fell to Earth as one.

But the air did not calm with their arrival. It did not return to normal until Alpha stood beside her mate with an army of Guardian beasts at her back.

"You called my dear?" she asked, letting her lips spread into a smile at his reaction to her arrival.

"Did you bring them all?" Omega questioned, raising his eyebrows in found amusement.

"Almost," Alpha replied. "Why did you call?" she asked, the question all were wanting answered.

The wolf turned to face Saul and the others before answering. "I believe Roman is here," he said, and watched for the reaction he knew would come.

He was not disappointed. Seven Immortal Guardians and a pack of beasts crouched as one and prepared to fight the Master of the Dark.

"Where?" Saul asked, letting his eyes roam the area. Peering into the deep shadows, but finding nothing to raise such an alarm.

"He's close!" Omega said. "Can't you smell him?"

"I can!" Jaxon said, not rising from his defensive stance. "The air is ripe with his stink. He must be close."

"He's with Haven and Wyatt," Hannah said, her eyes glowing a fierce red.

"But where?" Hunter asked, itching to find the Dark foe and do battle.

No answer was needed as a scream filled the night air and pointed the way for all to follow.

And they did.

As one, the Guardians moved towards the sound that did not fade away, but grew in agony and pain.

Omega shed his mortal form and led the charge, with Saul at his side and Callie on his shoulder. They found the small clearing in the few trees that dotted the plains and the sight that greeted them had all sucking in their breath in horror.

Wyatt stood to one side, casually donning his discarded clothes, until he was fully dressed and could lean back and watch what was to come next.

His first reaction at having the Dark Being appear over Haven's shoulder had made him gasp and fling himself from his lover, preparing to run.

But he didn't, as he recognized and bowed down to his master.

To Roman.

To the Dark.

To the power that was being offered to him.

He took it.

Chapter 49

Alpha and her beasts made ready to go to Wyatt but were stopped short at the bark from her mate.

"Stop!" Omega commanded, and crouched down on his belly as his hair made a ridge down his back and his fangs gleamed in the moonlight.

"Get back!" he growled, as he saw the Dark in the human and knew to go to him and offer protection would be folly.

Would be fatal.

He didn't want protection. Not from the Guardians. He wanted the Dark.

He hungered for the violence and death that the Dark Ones fed on.

He hungered for the power that the Dark whispered would be his if he only pledged his allegiance to Roman and his cause.

Roman saw the greed in Wyatt and he knew how to feed it and make it grow until the mortal was his for the taking.

Roman stood in the darkness of the night and he unleashed his power.

With fingers like dried twigs, with teeth grey with filth, and with dark whips of pain, he turned on the once favored minion of the Dark and he opened up the gates of hell to fuel his rage.

His fingers scored the now human flesh until it bled, not the black of the Dark but with the red of humanity.

His lips pulled back from his teeth and the jagged mass tasted the flesh that dared to defy him until he gorged himself on the tender treat.

Long spiked whips flew from his hands and beat at the body that jerked in pain at his feet. He gloried in the screams that were torn from Haven's throat every time they bit deep, until their echoes formed one long wail of agony.

He wanted Wyatt to see what was offered to him if he joined the Dark, and he was not disappointed. He watched as human eyes turned to black and the tongue, that wet the lips in pleasure, grew long and dark as it tried to catch the drops of red as they flew through the air like spring rain.

The Guardians and Immortal beasts sprang to attack, but the night was deep and the shadows vomited up waves of Dark Minions, willing to die to protect their master.

His back was guarded.

The attack stopped as suddenly as it had started.

Roman stood over the still human and watched as shallow breaths were fought for and achieved. But he knew it was not for long.

Roman turned his dark eyes, burning bright with fever, until they clashed and clung to his counter part from the light.

"Did you think I would not know what you were trying to do?" Roman asked, with his voice of wet ooze.

"I concede this one to you," he said, bowing at the waist and pointing his finger at the body of Haven. "But this one, this one is mine." All eyes turned to look at Wyatt as he inched closer and drank in the destruction at Romans feet.

"You have not won the battle yet!" Saul said, not giving Roman the satisfaction of admitting defeat. "And," Saul added, stopping Roman in his tracks as he turned to leave, "I will gladly take this one to a better place and teach her that kindness, goodness and love is still alive and well in this world and the next."

"Do what you want!" Roman sneered, not giving a damn if Haven's soul was saved or not. His work for the night was done and done well. Whether she knew it or not, liked it or not, his former minion had done exactly what he had wanted.

She had led Wyatt to the pool of Darkness and gotten him to drink deep of its foul waters.

"Go home!" Roman commanded and Wyatt did as he was told. He knew the mortal would not remember the details of this night, but he also knew that he would remember and want more.

More pain, more blood, more death.

"Any time you want to change sides," Roman taunted Ashton, "you know where to find me."

He disappeared along with his followers before the fire that flew from the Guardians hands could touch his being.

Only his laughter remained.

That sickening laughter and the tattered body of Haven.

Chapter 50

Saul moved to kneel down and smooth back the wet mass of hair that covered the torn face of Haven. He soothed her pain and made her passing one of gentleness and ease.

When the last sigh of breath passed the pale lips, Haven rose to stand beside the Guardians that watched with sorrow.

"Again?" she asked, rolling her eyes at her own death. "Wasn't once enough?" she asked her audience.

Dee went to her and wrapped the spirit in her arms and waited until arms rose and clasped her back. At first, with hesitation, not knowing how to respond to the kindness she could feel in Dee. Then with desperation at not wanting to let go of the only one who had ever held her with love.

"Saul?" Dee questioned and waited.

Omega moved to stand tall beside Saul before turning to Alpha and the beasts she had brought to fight. "I think your help is at an end for this night," he said to his mate and those that followed them.

"Very well," Alpha said, and watched as their army faded from sight. "What now?" she asked, wanting an answer along with the ones who remained.

All eyes turned to Saul and he gave it to them.

"Take her to the Gates," he said to Dee. "Tell them she has earned her rest."

Haven finally let her hold on Dee relax before moving to stand before Saul. She reached up with pale hands and pulled his head down to her waiting lips and placed a kiss of thanks on his Immortal cheek.

"Thank you," Haven said softly, the sound of tears in her voice. "I chose badly the first time and I never imagined I would get a chance to take it back."

The moon peered out from behind the scattering of clouds until a bright beam fell to Earth and lit the stairs that led up to the stars and beyond.

"Is that for me?" she asked, wondering at the unknown.

"It is,." Dee said, again standing at her side. "Take my hand and I will walk with you. We will make the journey together."

Haven took the offered hand and walked beside her Guardian, stopping with one foot on the first step. She turned back to look one last time at the beauty of the place she was leaving.

"He's not all bad you know," she said to them all. "Not yet. There's still a slim chance you can give Wyatt the chance you are giving me."

"You only get this chance when you have died," Dee explained. "Only then."

"I know," Haven said. "I know. But it's the only way you can save him. If you allow him to live, he will do Roman's bidding and many more will die. I'm telling you this so you can make a decision. A choice. Choose wisely." And with that she turned, and both ended and started her journey with Dee at her side.

When the moonlight once again returned to normal and the sounds of the night began again, six Immortal Guardians were left standing alone

They stood, deep in thought, until Dee came back to join them, before looking to their leader to say something.

"Well," Jaxon said "what's it going to be?"

"Not yet," Saul said to one and all. "We are not going to call the game just yet."

"It's not a game!" Hannah said, her eyes glowing deep red in the pre-dawn light.

"I know," Saul said wearily, a tired smile on his lips. "I will fight on. If you want to leave, any of you, I understand and will call if I need you."

"It's going to take more than just you to beat Roman," Hunter said, moving to Saul's side. "I'm in."

One by one they all moved to Saul's side, showing their support. Even Ashton, who would have liked nothing better than to end the battle now, as they all knew, moved silently to stand with Saul.

She didn't voice her opinion and she kept her feelings to herself. No matter how bitter of a taste it left in her mouth.

Maybe Saul was right. Maybe she harbored feelings against Wyatt because of what Leonard had done to her and Sam.

Maybe.

All she knew was this was going to end badly.

Very badly!

Chapter 51

Wyatt stirred in his bed as the morning sun burned through his window, letting him know it was well past dawn. He stretched and scratched until the blood began to flow in his veins and he gave his first thought to getting up and facing the day.

Rolling over and looking at his clock, his eyes popped open as he saw that it was past eight o'clock and he groaned, wondering how much trouble he was in for not helping with the morning chores.

Flopping back on his pillows, he snuggled down for five more minutes before he finally threw back the covers and headed for the bathroom.

Taking care of business, brushing the night breath from his mouth and pulling on his clothes, left him ready to make his way down the stairs and face his father's anger.

When he got to the kitchen all was quiet. No dad in sight.

He stood for just a few seconds, deciding what to do, before he heard a voice outside. He moved to the window to see who his father was talking to.

Wyatt's lip curled and his fists bunched as he looked out the window and saw his father sitting on the steps, talking to and petting his new best friend. That damned wolf!

Ethan had his arm around the animal's neck and wasn't paying attention to anything else. He missed when Floyd turned his head and stared through the window until Wyatt was sure he was looking right at him.

A growl rumbled through the house, but it wasn't the wolf that made the sound. It was Wyatt.

Omega did indeed look through the window until he found the eyes that had been boring a hole through him. His lip curled and, for a moment, he sneered at the boy and upon hearing the growl of anger from the human's throat, he let his lips tip up into a smile that taunted the teen and his reaction.

"Poor little human," he spoke to Wyatt's mind alone. "Did you think your father would not want a friend and companion he could rely on? One he could be himself with, and one who did not act like a spoiled brat whenever they were together. Did you think he would choose you over me? I see you did. How funny and naive you are."

Wyatt heard the words in his mind and he assumed it was he that had made up the conversation. He did not consider the wolf could speak to him.

No matter. Either way, Wyatt began to plot ways to rid the ranch, his father and himself of this presence until reaching his goal and the vermin's death was achieved.

Wyatt walked to the door and opened it, interrupting his father's conversation.

"Sorry I over slept," he began with insincerity, stretching his arms over his head. "Have you had breakfast yet?"

Ethan stopped in mid-sentence and looked back over his shoulder. His son looked as he always did, tall, handsome, strong and normal.

"He's not," a voice whispered in his ear. "He's not right! Beware!"

"Well that's just crazy!" Ethan thought to himself. *"He's my son. I've known him all his life."* But he knew the voice was on to something.

His son's eyes, which had always been the brightest of blues, were dull and shadowed today. Secrets seemed to move behind those eyes and the smile on his lips did not reach them to add warmth to their gaze.

Ethan shook himself to quiet his thoughts and pasted a smile of his own on his lips.

"As a matter of fact I haven't," he said, finally responding to his son's question. "I was waiting for you to get up and join me before I sat down to eat."

"Let's go in and get something now," Wyatt said, stepping aside and swinging the door wider in invitation.

Ethan nodded his head and rose to his feet. Before he could take a step, Floyd made a dash for the door, intending to enter the house and stay close to the human he felt needed his protection.

Before he could get past Wyatt the boy's foot lashed out and connected with his side and brought a yelp of surprise and pain from the wolf's throat.

Vengeance was born in the Immortal Beast and his teeth grew long and deadly with his intent.

Before he could act, Ethan moved to stand between the two and bent over to run a hand over the injured wolf's side.

"What the hell was that for?" Ethan asked, frowning and shocked at the action his son had performed.

"Since when is it okay for him to come into the house?" Wyatt demanded, blocking the way inside with his body.

"We let Gabriel in the house all the time." Ethan replied, stroking his friend to ease the pain.

"This is not Gabriel," Wyatt sneered, willing to argue the point further. "I don't think it's a good idea to start letting him get comfortable coming in."

"I don't know why you don't like him, and don't say you do because I can see you don't. But it's still my house and I say he can come in!" Ethan lectured angrily, muscling past his son and clearing a path for Floyd to enter unharmed.

Floyd walked past Ethan and licked his hand in gratitude, but his eyes still shone bright with anger. He was far from letting the incident go unpunished.

"You have to sleep sometime," Omega thought, swallowing the retaliation he had in mind. "It better be with one eye open little one, because my memory is long. Very long and I never forget!" he promised. He could wait.

Alpha and Callie would not.

Chapter 52

Alpha had stayed close by, even after Omega had turned back into the wolf at dawn's first light. She did not like the smell of Darkness and death that had clung to the human boy. She was angered that he had not lifted a finger to help when Haven had been attacked.

She knew the Dark had its claws deep into this young human and she feared for her mate. Though she would never tell him so, still it never hurt to have an extra pair of eyes to watch his back.

Callie and she had been laying in the sun as Ethan had stroked and talked to Omega, keeping watch for anything that dared to move in the morning shadows.

But things were quiet. All had been well until the boy came out onto the porch. Alpha's ears had perked up and she rose to her feet as she saw the hatred in his eyes for her mate.

When the door had been opened wide and Omega had tried to enter, Alpha knew rage as she saw the kick he received.

Her teeth were bared as she began to inch unseen across the yard, intending to leap upon the Dark One and find pleasure in allowing her jaws to clamp around the puny human throat until its neck snapped in her mouth.

Before she could complete her plan Ethan had intervened and the door had been closed in her snarling face. Not that that would have stopped her if she wanted in, but she stood down, knowing Omega had a champion in the father.

Callie stood beside the Mother of all Animals hissing and spitting in shared anger until Alpha shook her head and stalked back down the stairs.

"This cannot go unpunished!" the wee Guardian said in a voice low and deep.

"Agreed," Alpha said, walking back to her place in the sun and laying down to think.

Snickers and laughter came from the thin shadows as Dark Minions showed their amusement at the beasts as they lay in the sun.

Alpha took it for as long as she could before reacting with the speed of light. Catching the 'too slow' Dark Ones in her death dealing jaws, she chewed and snapped until the few that escaped did so with great speed, not wanting their blood to join the already thick stream flowing from the female's mouth.

"Don't come back!" she growled with menace, before cleaning her face of the stench the Dark blood carried.

"What are you planning?" Callie asked, as the great she beast lifted her head to the skies and sent out a call.

"Just a small bit of mischief," Alpha said, as a smile curved her beautiful mouth. "Nothing that could lead back to Omega."

Callie ruffled her small wings and moved to sit by her partner in crime and wait.

She didn't have to wait long.

A small dark speck on the horizon formed and grew until, along with the cloud, hundreds of voices could be heard honking in conversation.

Callie looked to Alpha, waiting for an explanation, but the Mother of all Beasts just sat down and watched what was about to happen.

The cloud of migrating Canadian geese drew nearer, until they made a sweeping arch and dove low towards the ground.

It only took seconds until Callie was made aware of the revenge Alpha had planned for Wyatt.

As each goose flew over the yard, they deposited their "load" until Wyatt's nice, clean pick up was covered in goose poop from head lights to tail gate. The pretty clean vehicle was no more. In its stead sat a green, runny mass of crap that would dry long before Wyatt knew what hit him or rather his pick up.

Callie's small voice trickled out as she laughed in shocked amusement. Alpha was not so quiet.

She rolled onto her back and kicked her feet towards the sky as she roared with laughter.

"Thank you!" she gasped to her avengers, receiving honks of "you're welcome!" before they flew out of sight.

"Well?" she asked Callie when she could control herself once more.

"Brilliant!" Callie replied, her eyes bright with mirth. "It will take him hours to clean the dried mess from his prized possession. I simply love it!"

Before Alpha could continue the conversation, the door to the house opened and the target of Alpha's mischief came out. Alpha watched in silence as the boy stopped and stared at the mess in the yard.

Once again, she howled with laughter as he screamed in rage. Both Guardians watched as he ran to his vehicle and danced around it in anger, turning the air blue with his foul cuss words.

The door opened again and spit out both Ethan and Omega as they came to see what the commotion was all about.

Ethan stopped with his mouth open for just a moment, before covering the said portal to hide his smile of amusement so as not to add fuel to the fire his son was already burning with.

Omega looked around the yard with his Immortal eyes until he spotted Alpha and Callie sitting in the sun, each rolling with glee, and he knew what had happened and why.

Sitting down on his butt, he let his tongue loll out and his eyes of silver became bright with appreciation and humor.

He huffed out a breath, drawing the attention of Ethan until he reached out a hand and stroked the wolf at his side.

"Well crap!" Ethan said under his breath for Floyd alone to hear, before having to laugh at the pun he had not intended.

"Make sure you wash that off down beside the barn," he warned his son. "I don't want an ice puddle in the yard."

"Aren't you going to help?" Wyatt asked, thinking his father should lend a hand out of kindness.

"Nope," Ethan said, before snapping his fingers and inviting Floyd to come back inside with him.

Before he complied Omega, not Floyd, looked back over his shoulder and let his lip curl with contempt.

Wyatt saw and kicked dirt in the direction of the now closed door.

Alpha growled.

Chapter 53

It took Wyatt all afternoon to clean the green, dried goose poop from his ride and then he had to wax it, as the acid from the mess had left dull spots in the finish. Well pretty much the whole thing, as he didn't think there had been an inch of metal left exposed after the birds' attack.

Geese were the devils spawn, he was now sure, and he itched to grab a gun and go hunting the useless birds into extinction.

Throwing the dirty rags in a heap against the barn, he kicked some loose leaves over them and left them there, knowing his father would find them later. That's what he got for not helping him, Wyatt reasoned.

Pulling his vehicle back to the front of the house, Wyatt got out and made ready to mount the steps and enter the house. He was hungry, thirsty and cold and in no mood to play nice with anyone.

He stopped at the bottom step and looked at the wolf that lay on the porch with his eyes open to mere slits as he enjoyed the afternoon's direct sunlight.

Wyatt stood still as he imagined having the chance to get the wolf in his gun's sight and pulling the trigger. Thoughts of revenge on the pooping flock of geese were pushed from his mind as a bloodlust filled him for the wolf, and him alone.

"You may think you're safe." Wyatt said, as he walked up the steps to the door. "But you're not. Not as long as I'm here!" he said and hawked a loogie of spit in the direction of Floyd.

Silver eyes opened wide as the glob of spit landed mere inches from his face. They held no warmth for the human boy that carried the Darkness within him.

Silver turned to molten metal and his fangs grew until his lips no longer covered them.

"Keep it up brat boy!" the wolf thought to himself. *"I'm not going anywhere, but in time you will. In time Karma is going to show up on your door step and bite you in the ass! Hard!"* He let his long tongue creep out and lick his lips in anticipation of the event.

Wyatt watched the wolf lick his lips and a small trickle of fear traveled his spine, until the hair on his arms stood up and he shivered with something other than the cold.

"Screw you!" he said with false bravado, before hurrying into the house and jerking the door closed behind him.

Omega laid his head back on his great paws and chuckled under his breath. Revenge was sweet and he knew the time would come for him to taste it until he had his fill.

Callie watched all from her perch upon Omega's shoulders and her growl at the sight was deep. She knew, as they all did, that the cleansing of the Dark each night was doing no good.

Soon would come the time that the towel would have to be thrown in and this mortal's soul would be lost to the side of good. But that time was not yet. If there was even a glimmer of hope then the Guardians would continue to fight, they would fight because Saul asked it of them.

She waited until Omega calmed himself and closed his eyes to rest his mortal form before traveling into the house to see what was happening.

Should the need to protect Ethan arise, she would sound the alarm and summon help to make sure he was safe from the evil that he had no idea lived under his very roof.

It was a good thing she did

But it was not Ethan that needed protection.

Chapter 54

Wyatt walked into the kitchen and found his father sitting at the table reading the paper as if nothing had happened.

No, "how did it go?"

No, "sorry I didn't come help you."

No words of any kind came from his father. He just sat there and ignored him.

Wyatt burned!

Before Wyatt could say anything, Ethan folded the paper with a snap and rose to walk to the cupboard. Pulling out a bag of dog food, he began to prepare a bowl of food for Floyd for his lunch.

"He gets that damn wolf some food but I have to get my own?" Wyatt thought to himself. *"That's bull!"*

Before he could pour, Ethan's phone rang and he set the bag down to answer it.

From his end, Wyatt figured it was one of the neighbors calling to ask his dad advice on a problem and, just like that, the feeding was put aside.

As Ethan walked away, Wyatt had an idea. He took his fathers place and poured the food into the waiting dish. At Ethan's questioning look, Wyatt told him, "I'll take care of feeding the animal."

Ethan shrugged his shoulders and moved off to continue his conversation, leaving Wyatt alone.

Except for Callie.

Callie watched the boy and her back arched as she watched him bend down and rummage through the doors under the sink until he found a bottle and stand back up.

She moved closer and watched as Wyatt poured some kind of liquid over the food before stirring it with a spoon and adding more food on top.

"I hope this doesn't kill you too fast," the boy said under his breath, sure no one was listening.

"I hope you die a long, slow, painful death," Wyatt muttered, a smile of satisfaction and anticipation curving his mouth.

Callie followed him as he walked out with the bowl and set it within reach of the wolf's mouth.

"Eat up," Wyatt crooned, as the nose began to twitch and Floyd rose to his feet to eat.

"Don't!" Callie roared

Immortal eyes of silver looked until they found the small Guardian and the hungry mouth closed before it took a bite.

"What is it little one?" Omega questioned her.

"The boy has put something in the food to kill your mortal form," Callie said, her voice heavy with anger. "Beware!"

Wyatt watched as the wolf casually walked down the steps, dug a hole with his powerful front paws. He watched as the beast came back to nudge the dish to the edge of the porch until it spilled over the side and emptied its contents into that same hole.

He watched as the wolf again used his front paws to send the dirt flying until the food was covered up and presented a danger no more to himself or another that would come to feast upon the food.

Wyatt's anger exploded as the wolf, with a final act of defiance, lifted his leg and peed on the mound of fresh dirt, taking his time until he was finished.

Omega walked on quiet feet until he again stood upon the porch and faced his enemy. But he did not stand tall. Instead he crouched low to the floor and looked at his attacker, with eyes that glowed and ears laid flat against his skull.

His lips curled back and showed teeth long and sharp as a deep, ugly growl rumbled in his chest and he dared the human to act.

"Feeling froggy?" Omega asked, even though the human ears could not hear him. "If you are then by all means jump," he taunted, never taking his eyes from the boy.

Omega watched as Wyatt's hands curled into fists and the mortal took a step forward to start a battle

"Not yet." a voice whispered in Wyatt's ear. "You must be slyer than this if you want to win and kill your prey," the Dark voice instructed.

Omega and Callie heard the voice that spoke to Wyatt and Callie sent out a call for the Guardians to come and come now.

Roman had arrived.

Chapter 55

They came!

All of them!

Landing in the yard with a howl of wind from Immortal wings, seven Guardians formed a line and prepared for battle.

"Come to play?" Ashton asked the Dark Being that stood behind the human boy.

Roman giggled as he looked upon the Guardians that dared to challenge him.

"I don't play," he said, slowly swaying from side to side, still using the boy as a shield. "This one is mine. Why do you persist when you know this is the truth?"

"Just to piss you off!" Jaxon said, dry humor in his voice. He looked around the yard and could not see any of Roman's minions hiding in wait. It wasn't like the Leader of the Dark to come alone and show himself when he was out numbered.

"I don't need my followers to do what needs to be done here," Roman said, knowing what Jaxon was looking for, seeking out.

"I think you're finished here," Saul said, stepping in front of his friends.

"Think so?" Roman threw back at him. "I will wager that you and your little band of 'do-gooders' are the ones finished here today."

Hunter and Jaxon took a step closer and Roman wagged a dirty finger at them.

"No closer," he commanded "or things will happen that none of you want to be a part of. Not today anyway."

Omega waited until Roman's attention was centered on the Guardians before taking his true form. He rose up tall and powerful, preparing to leap at the wisp of smoke and hold him in his jaws until the others could move in.

"Bad dog!" Roman said, swinging his black eyes to pin the beast in place. "Keep that up and I will teach you to play dead. For real!"

Saul held up his hand to halt the attack and moved to stand at the bottom of the porch steps.

"You are done here!" Saul said, feeling confident that Roman was doing no more than playing with them. "Be gone from here before you lose your life over one soul that you have no need for."

"But I want this one!" Roman said, moving back from Wyatt. "I own this one because he has had a taste of me and my kind and he likes it. He was made for it. I recognize a hunger for the Dark when I see it and this one is and will be mine."

"Then you leave me no choice," Saul said, as he unfurled his wings of white. "You leave me no choice this day but to fight!"

In the blink of an eye Roman moved.

He dove into Wyatt and Saul could do nothing about it.

To fight Roman now would mean he would have to kill Wyatt to get the Dark One to leave his body. Saul was not prepared to do that.

Roman had won.

For now.

With the voice of the human Roman laughed.

Chapter 56

The stunned Guardians stood still as stone as Wyatt jerked and danced as if on the end of an electrical live wire. It only took seconds, but that was enough.

When Wyatt stilled, he lifted his head from his chest and looked with eyes of true black out to where the Immortal Guardians stood.

He saw them. He saw them all through Roman's eyes. Eyes that were now his.

"I don't understand," he said to the new room mate in his head. "What's happening?"

"Don't you know me?" Roman asked with a voice as smooth as fresh oil. "Let me show you," he said and pulled memories from Wyatt's mind of times when shadows had moved and darkness had whispered to him.

"That was you?" the boy asked, still not fully understanding what it all meant. "What are you? Who are you?"

Roman huffed out a breath at the slowness of the human mind and clamped down on his impatience, not wanting to turn his new home against him. He wanted to stay for awhile and had every intention of doing so.

He looked out at the Guardians and knew as long as he had control of Wyatt they were powerless to act against him. Now if it was him on the outside and Saul had pulled what he did, he would not have hesitated in striking down the mortal and forcing the Guardian back out into the open.

That was the difference between the Dark and the Guardians. He would not hesitate to kill and they did. "Fools!" he laughed. "Stupid fools!"

Roman's concentration was brought back to Wyatt when the body began to get antsy as he failed to answer the questions right away.

"You ask me who I am. I am Roman. I am the leader of all that goes bump in the night. I am the leader of an army bigger than you can imagine."

"We are the ones that spread hate, discontent, chaos and death on this sewer called Earth."

"We are the ones that cause good men to go bad. The leaders of great countries that live for greed, power and no one but themselves are the product of our labors."

"We are mighty! We are legion! We are the Dark and we are unstoppable!"

"What do you want with me?" Wyatt asked, still not understanding why he was having a conversation in his head with a voice only he could hear.

"Yes, tell him what plans you have for his soul," Saul said in a smooth coaxing tone, stepping forward drawing the eyes of black to him.

"Tell him that you plan to use him for, for lack of a better word, Evil. Tell him that when you are done with him you will drag his soul down into the Dark and let him rot there until you remember him and order him to do your bidding," Saul concluded.

"Who the hell are you?" Wyatt asked, as feelings of hate rose up inside him until his throat was clogged with the bile of Darkness.

"You might say I am Roman's opposite," Saul began, dipping his head as he spoke. "My name is Saul, and the ones here with me are just a few of my warriors fighting for the side of good."

"Boring!" Roman's voice sing-songed in Wyatt's head.

"You have a choice," Saul said, speaking to the remaining humanity in the boy standing before him.

"You can choose to resist the Darkness hiding in you," The leader of the Guardians said as Sam, Ashton, Hunter, Dee, Hannah and Jaxon began to slowly fan out behind him.

Six sets of impressive wings slowly opened until their tips touched and left the human with his mouth open in awe.

"Wow!" Wyatt breathed out. "You all look like super heroes!" he said, clearly proving he was still a kid at heart.

Wyatt let his eyes travel the ones standing in the yard and he judged them as he did.

He took in the strength of Jaxon and Hunter and knew they would not spare his life if a battle took place.

He looked into eyes that glowed like fire from Hannah and he felt the power of Dee as she inched her way into his mind.

With Sam, he sensed cunning and knew he killed with cold calculated skill.

But it was Ashton that made him stop and stare the longest.

He saw her standing with the others and he watched, in fascination, as fire danced from her hands, itching to escape. He liked the long dark hair that flowed down her back and he wondered what it would be like to have her as a friend and ally.

"Dream on!" Ashton said, reading the look of interest in the black eyes.

"This spirit knows you," Roman said with conviction and wondered at the young mortal's fascination.

"Yeah we have a history," Ashton supplied without warmth.

Roman shrugged his mortal shoulders and moved on. It made no difference to him what Wyatt did or did not want. He was in control now and he always got his way.

"Well, it's been nice talking to you, but I really have things to do. So tah tah for now," Roman said, wagging his fingers in farewell.

He turned to enter the house, keeping his eyes on the Immortal Beast at his side.

"Be gone when I come back out!" he warned, sure his words would be obeyed.

"Bite me!" Omega said, sitting down to let Roman know he was staying.

"Don't say I didn't warn you," the Dark One threw over his shoulder before entering the house and shutting the door.

"Callie!" Saul commanded. "Stay close to Wyatt when he is around his father. If he tries to harm Ethan sound the alarm."

Callie nodded her head and disappeared into the house, leaving the rest to stand looking at Saul.

"We need to make a decision," Jaxon said, his stance straight and tall, muscles flexed.

"Are you sure you want to stay?" Saul asked the Father of all Beasts.

"I stay!" Omega said, as he snapped his jaws tight with anger.

"Very well," Saul said, leaving it at that. "The rest of you, come with me," he commanded before leaping into the air.

Seven pairs of wings pushed down hard until the wind screamed with the force they generated.

The yard became quiet, with nothing left moving except the wolf that now lay down to wait.

But he would not wait long.

"Come on out and play you black devil," the wolf said, as he raised his nose into the air and cried the long eerie song of his kind.

The battle cry had been given and his warriors responded until every tree and every bush had eyes in them and his back was well covered.

Omega may have stayed behind, but he would not stay alone.

Sharp claws and teeth hid, ready to rend the dark flesh of any that dared to threaten their leader.

Growls of anticipation were kept quiet until one by one the Dark followers came to populate the growing shadows, feeling bold as evening approached.

They came, but none of them would leave.

Hungry beasts fed until their bellies were sated with the flesh of the Dark. Jaws were licked and claws were cleaned until the evidence of the carnage was wiped clean.

Omega burped.

Chapter 57

Saul did not immediately join his friends on their mountain top. He needed time to think. Come up with a plan. But could he?

Now that Roman literally had his claws in Wyatt, Saul could see no way to pry them loose without ending the mortal life of Leonard's soul.

Saul stood before The Window to the World for but a moment of his time, but on Earth, in Wyatt's life, days and weeks flew by.

Saul watched as the boy became a beacon for the Dark. He watched as Wyatt became a bully, a thief and a whiney brat that could only say "me me me" about every thing life gave to him.

All the lessons on how to be a good man and a good human being that his father tried to teach him fell on deaf ears and a cold dark heart.

Saul had no answers.

The winds stirred and a quiet thud had Saul turning from the Window.

"What is it Dee?" Saul asked, with defeat in his voice.

"I have someone here that would like to speak to you," the Guardian said, stepping aside until Saul could see who stood hidden behind the great expanse of her wings.

Saul looked upon the woman coming towards him and did not recognize her as one of his own.

"What is this?" he asked Dee, totally at a loss.

"Not what, but who," Dee said, giving him a sweet smile of encouragement.

"I see you do not remember me," the woman said in a quiet voice. "My name is Mattie. I'm Wyatt's mother." she said, dropping the information bomb at Saul's feet.

Saul's brows rose in disbelief, as he stood preparing to talk to the dead woman.

"I don't understand," he said, after he had a moment to gather his thoughts. "We took you to the gates. You walked through the gates. How is it you can come back through when no one has been able to before?"

Mattie moved slowly until she stood beside Saul. But rather than face him she looked into the Window and saw her boy. Her son Wyatt. She saw him acting as she would never have believed possible. He truly was a brutal, selfish brat.

Her heart hurt, for the love she still carried for her child still filled it, and the one she watched now was a stranger to her. All she had hoped he would become was not the reality of this young man's life.

"That's my boy?" she asked Saul, reaching out a hand that longed to touch him just once.

"I'm sorry," Saul said. "I'm sorry for your loss. Not the loss of your life, but for the loss of a loved one whose destiny was derailed by the Dark."

Mattie nodded her head in understanding and a lone tear crept down her pale cheek.

"I know you and your kind escort us to the gates and must leave us there. But those of us on the other side get to see glimpses of our loved ones as they live until they join us," Mattie said, giving him some background information.

"I've been able to see what has happened to my son. I've also been granted a favor to come here and speak with you about Wyatt," she concluded.

"What can I do for you?" Saul asked, feeling this was going to be a waste of her time and his.

"I have come here to ask you to save my son," Mattie said, finally turning to look the Immortal Guardian straight in the eye.

Saul was quiet for a time before looking to Dee for assistance in telling her they had lost him to the Dark.

Dee watched as Saul's strong shoulders slumped in defeat, and she almost looked away from the eyes that carried nothing of the hope Mattie was looking for.

"We tried," Saul said, with gentle compassion in his voice. "We have tried to find a way to force the Dark from inside Wyatt, but we have failed."

"I am at a loss for an answer as to what to do now," he admitted, though the words were bitter on his tongue and the lie burned in his gut.

"No you're not," Mattie replied, her blue eyes growing stormy with her emotions. "You know what needs to be done and I'm asking you to do it! Spare my husband the pain of what Wyatt will do once he is out of the house and on his own," she said, with a loving wife's passion. "The loss of our son will hurt him. But the burden of what Wyatt will do will eat his soul until he will go crazy with guilt and self doubt."

Saul had opened his mouth to answer this mother, but before he could speak she gave him one last thought on the matter.

"Kill him," Mattie said, grabbing the Guardian's arm in a grip of steel. "Kill him! Kill Wyatt!"

Saul walked away.

Chapter 58

Mattie watched as Saul kept walking until he was out of sight. "What now?" she asked Dee, with a look of confusion on her lovely face.

"How is it that you, a mother, can ask such a thing of the Guardians?" Dee asked, shocked at what she had just witnessed. "I thought a mother would fight with everything in her power to protect her children. Again, why is it you ask this of us?"

Mattie did not hang her head in shame for her request. Instead she stood tall with fire in her eyes and her fists clenched at her sides.

"I have been shown what Wyatt will become if someone, if you, the Guardians, do not act and do it quickly. I have seen the death and sadness he will be responsible for if Roman is allowed to continue to lead him to do his bidding."

"How can I not ask you to remedy this situation before it becomes unbearable to not only Ethan, but to every life

Wyatt will touch? How can I let this go on unchecked?" she asked with desperation in her voice.

Dee was silent.

"I was told," Mattie began again, taking Dee's hand in her own, "that the Guardians of humanity were unwilling to take the steps that were needed to deny the Dark a new weapon. Wyatt will be that weapon if something is not done and done quickly."

"I needed to come to you, and to Saul, to let you know I understand what needs to be done. If you need to hear these words then here they are. I forgive you."

"I forgive you," Mattie said again, making sure Dee heard her and knew her words to be true.

"We do not need your forgiveness," Dee said, wondering where this spirit had gotten the idea that Guardians needed such a thing.

"Saul does," Mattie said. "He feels he has failed with my son's soul and he fights on when he knows in his heart that to do so is futile."

"I have come today to give him permission to do the right thing and spare many lives by ending Wyatt's."

"Wyatt may not be allowed to come to you after his human death," Dee said, making sure Mattie understood the consequences of her request.

"Yes, I know," Mattie said, showing the first sign that her actions on this day cost her something. Sadness bloomed in her eyes and Dee knew she wanted to wail out her deep sorrow for what her son had become.

Dee waited in silence, waiting to see what Mattie would do.

"I know I may never have the chance to meet my son and hold him in my arms," the spirit said quietly. "But I will be able to have Ethan by my side one day, and we will hold each other and heal the sorrow and pain of losing Wyatt in our spirits together."

"Why has this happened?" Mattie asked of Dee. "Why Wyatt?"

Dee started to walk and motioned Mattie to join her before she began to speak.

"Wyatt's soul is old," the Guardian said. "This is not the first time it has been born into a human body."

"The last time Leonard, as he was known before, passed, he was given the chance to be a Guardian and he ended up causing the premature death of a woman. Her destiny and that of her soul's mate were changed, cheated of a life they were supposed to live together."

"Saul had to step in and repair the damage as best he could, but Leonard was not allowed to return to Earth until he had learned his lessons and then you had been blessed with a baby."

"Roman, the leader of the Dark, wanted him, this soul, and waited until he was born again. He now has the chance to turn him away from his destiny and use him as a human soldier for the Dark."

"We have been working to give Wyatt a chance at the life he was to lead but Roman has entered the boy and now leads him from within. We are losing him," Dee finished with a long sigh.

Mattie walked in silence for a time before stopping. She waited for Dee to do the same and stand beside her before speaking.

"I now see why you fight so hard for my son," she said, with a sad smile. "But the facts are still the same. Roman has my son and you must do what needs to be done to save as many of his would be victims from him as you can."

"I need you to go to Saul and tell him what I have said today!" she implored. "Do not take no for an answer. This must be done!"

Dee opened her mouth to respond, but Mattie tilted her head and spoke first.

"My time is at an end," she said. "I have to go."

"Should I take you back?" Dee asked, but did not need an answer as Mattie's form began to fade.

"I'll be watching," Mattie said before she disappeared for good.

Dee needed to go find the others and tell them what had happened before they went to Saul as one.

She spread her wings and headed towards the meeting spot of her friends on the mountain top, calling them to her as she went.

A decision had to be made once and for all. But she didn't like their choices.

None of them would.

Chapter 59

Dee waited until all were present before relaying to them the strange meeting she and Saul had just had with Mattie.

Hunter whistled through his teeth when Dee was finished and all had fallen quiet.

"You talked with a ghost?" he asked, in total awe. "Cool!"

Hannah rolled her unusual eyes and shook her dark head at Hunter's enthusiasm.

"Why are you so impressed?" Hannah asked. "We see ghosts everyday, all day, everywhere. What's the big deal with this one?"

Hunter walked over to Dee and looped a loving arm around her neck until she was snuggled against his side before answering.

"True," he said. "but not the ones who have passed on to live beyond the Great Gates. The ones we see are the ones that refuse to leave for whatever reason. This Mattie is the only one I have heard of that has come back from beyond the Gates."

"And her request is highly unusual!" Jaxon supplied for them all.

"A mother does not find us and ask that we kill her son every day," Sam said, joining in.

"It hurt her to ask this of us," Dee said softly. "I could feel her pain."

"Still it's a good plan," Ashton said, no indecision in her voice. "It is, I believe, the only course of action left to us if we intend to protect the rest of mankind from Roman and what he has planned."

"We can continue to watch and thwart whatever Wyatt tries," Sam said, giving them more options to think about.

"Do we want to waste the time it would take to do this?" Hannah posed the question.

"I think we must give it one last try before we throw in the towel," Jaxon agreed, looking at each Guardian for confirmation. Four heads nodded in agreement, leaving only Ashton standing alone with her arms crossed over her chest.

Sam went to her and gently rubbed her back, trying to ease the tension there.

"We must try one more time before we go to Saul," he said quietly in her ear. "If it doesn't work then we will act on Mattie's request. Agreed?" he asked, waiting for Ashton to nod her head.

Ashton did not want to agree to this plan. She wanted to be done with this mess once and for all. She wanted Leonard done once and for all!

She knew all along that he was bad and she was surprised that the others could not see it as well. Whether it was due to denial or ignorance, the truth was still the same.

The fire in her licked at her fingers and it wanted to be let loose until it could burn to ashes the soul Roman now controlled. But, for Sam and the others, she got control and finally gave her consent.

"I'm in," she said to Sam reluctantly. "Only because you asked it of me," she paused, "I'm in."

Sam let out the breath he was holding and turned to the others with purpose.

"It is agreed that we will give it one last try," he said, taking charge. "I think it would be best to guard in pairs. This will allow one to stay with Wyatt while the other can warn his intended victim and make sure no harm is done."

"Sounds good to me," Jaxon said, approving Sam's plan. "Hannah and I will take the first watch."

"Then it's agreed. When we are done we will call the next pair to us and fill them in on what has been happening," Hannah concluded.

Grabbing Hannah's hand, Jaxon opened his wings and together they leapt into the air to find Wyatt and put this last ditch effort into effect.

Ashton felt a twinge of guilt at not speaking up to alert the others to a flaw she could see in the plan. In fact she was rather surprised that none of the others had thought of it but her.

Since Roman now resided inside Wyatt, the boy could see the Guardians through his eyes. How were they supposed to keep an eye on him and protect those he would harm if he and Roman could see them?

Just being there was not going to be enough. She doubted that Roman would do what he was going to do if he could see them. Which Ashton figured would just have them following Wyatt around like little puppies and rendering them ineffective. Then again, if it kept Roman from using Wyatt to do harm to others it would accomplish something worth while.

Shrugging her shoulders, she kept her doubts to herself. After all Hannah and Jaxon were pretty smart cookies and would probably come up with a fix for them all to follow.

One more chance.

One more chance to save a soul.

Time would tell.

Chapter 60

Ashton had hit the nail right on the head.

Wyatt knew the second the pair appeared. But this time he was not in awe of the winged figures that watched him.

His new master had given him the knowledge of who and what these Immortal Guardians were and he was not impressed.

Roman had whispered to him, showing him the power he now shared with the Dark Master. Wyatt now knew he was a match for any that would do Roman or himself harm. As long as he accepted the Dark One and followed his orders he would be protected.

"We have company," Roman whispered in Wyatt's mind.

"Yes I see them," Wyatt whispered back. "What do they want? What should I do?" he asked.

Roman was quiet for a moment before whispering to the boy a plan he came up with. Wyatt smiled to himself and followed his master's instructions.

The bell rang, causing Wyatt and the other students to head towards the door and the next classes they had to attend.

Jaxon and Hannah tagged along, unaware they had been detected.

They stayed by the boy until the long afternoon was at an end and they could finally leave the building and head to the farm where they assumed Wyatt would go.

Hunter and Dee met them as they landed away from the house and the four stood with their heads together, talking and planning.

Time passed until the shadows of the dying sun became long and, as one earth hour passed, Jaxon and Hunter began to itch with the feeling something was wrong.

"Where is he?" Hunter asked, giving voice to Jaxon's thoughts.

Dee and Hannah became still as they too got the feeling they had been duped.

"We assumed he was coming home," Hannah said to Jaxon before looking at the others.

The low hum of a vehicle approaching had them turning to watch as Wyatt finally pulled into the yard and they waited until he shut the motor off and opened the door. They moved closer.

Floyd lifted his head and sniffed the air from the porch where he had taken up watch when Ethan had gone inside.

The hair on his back rose and his nose wrinkled as a growl rumbled in his chest. Lips pulled back until long teeth could be seen and his ears lay flat on his head

"I smell death," the wolf said to the Guardians standing by the pickup. "He stinks of death."

Wyatt closed the door and turned to stare straight at Jaxon.

"You missed all the fun," the boy said with a sassy smile. "Too bad you had to sit through classes and not get to have even a little bit of fun for your troubles."

"What did we miss?" Hunter asked, drawing the attention of Wyatt.

"Why if I tell you that would ruin all our fun!" the mortal crowed. "I guess you will just have to wait to find out like all the rest. It shouldn't be long though" Wyatt threw over his shoulder, placing his foot on the first step of the porch.

Floyd moved on stiff legs to block his ascent, but before he could emit a growl of warning, the door opened with a bang and Ethan came charging out.

"Get in the truck!" he ordered Wyatt on the run.

"What for?" Wyatt asked, feigning confusion.

"They found a body out in a pasture. One of the kids from school is what I heard. We're going to see if we can help!" Ethan barked, yanking the truck door open and sliding into the driver's seat.

Floyd jumped off the porch and in one fluid motion landed in the bed, declaring to all he was going with.

"I will tell you what I see," he said to the Guardians already preparing to join him.

"Let him go," Dee said to Hunter and Jaxon as she could see they wanted to ride with the wolf. "There's nothing we can do now but stand by and watch. We all know who is responsible for the death and we need to go to Saul and fill him in."

Jaxon's arms bulged with the restraint he held himself under. It was all Hunter could do to hold him back when Wyatt looked at them with a smug smirk on his face and a wink from his black eyes before joining his father.

The dust still filled the air from the churning tires when Hunter let Jaxon go and, as one, the four Immortals shot into the air like guided missiles.

"We are going to see what happened before everyone gets there," Jaxon said. "I want to see!"

No one argued with him as they too wanted to see first hand what had happened.

A small crowd of people had gathered on the edge of a small clump of trees before the Guardians joined them with a swirl of dust and a gust of wind.

Jaxon looked on the carnage before turning to Hannah and spoke.

"Tell Omega to get out," he said. "Tell him his work here is finished."

Hannah nodded her head and left to intercept the Leader of all Animals before he could walk into Roman's trap.

She found the truck speeding down the road about a mile from the scene and, with a gentle thump, came to rest beside the wolf.

"You have to leave," she said, resting her hand on the great beast's shoulders.

Floyd licked his lips and looked up at Hannah. "What are you talking about?" he asked, seeing the look of concern in her deep red eyes.

"It's a trap!" Hannah said, her dark hair streaming out behind her. "Wyatt has set a trap for you. Your work here is over."

"Tell me!" the Immortal Beast demanded.

"I only looked for a second, but the body is ripped to shreds. As if attacked by an animal. As if attacked by a wolf," she finished, watching for Omega to appear.

She was not disappointed.

Where the mortal body of a wolf had been there now stood the proud and noble form of Omega in all his Immortal glory.

A mortal wolf may have been in danger from the fear of the humans but Omega was not.

Omega feared no man. He feared no being from the Dark either.

He lowered his great head until his eyes could see into the cab and they zeroed in on Wyatt.

He snapped his jaws and thumped his nose against the window until the boy and his Dark master turned to look over their shoulder at him.

Looked over their shoulder into the face of death.

Roman squealed.

The Beast laughed.

Chapter 61

Ethan pulled his truck in beside the ones already forming a line and got out.

"Let's go!" he ordered, not giving Wyatt a chance to stay where he was.

Wyatt did not argue as he looked one more time at the beast in the bed of the truck. He felt Roman's fear, so he did not have to be told twice to follow his father.

"Why do you fear this one?" Wyatt asked Roman, as he followed his father until they reached the edge of the small crowd.

"Omega and his pack are different," Roman said, hiding in Wyatt's mind. "They do not fight as Saul and his army do. They bite and claw and chew until their foes are nothing but chunks of flesh or piles of ash. They destroy all that stand against them or do harm to mortal animals. They bring death to the Dark Ones."

"Why don't they hunt the Guardians also?" Wyatt asked, thinking that if they could get them on their side then they would be unstoppable.

"The Guardians do not hurt humans, nor do they harm animals unless they themselves are dark and evil. Only when a Guardian turns to the Dark, only then do the Beasts hunt and kill those on the side of good. Otherwise they stay out of our fight and care only for their own kind."

Wyatt forgot the conversation as he stood with his father, stood close enough to see what was left of the body on the grassy, cold ground.

It was unclear whether it was a boy or a girl that lay in a mauled heap. The grass, that should have been brown with the winter kill, was now stained a rusty red and lay flat against the earth where the killing had taken place.

Wyatt stared in sick fascination, wondering what had done this.

"Don't you remember?" Roman whispered, opening a door in the boys mind.

And Wyatt did.

Memories flooded him until his head reeled with the feelings, the sights, the sounds and the smells murder carried with it.

Wyatt remembered picking up the young boy along side the road as he walked home from school.

He remembered driving him to a spot some ways down the road and pulling over, telling the youth he wanted to show him something.

He remembered the boy getting out and telling him how he had always looked up to the popular Wyatt and he almost danced to his death as he followed Wyatt like an obedient puppy.

He remembered the boy screaming as Roman turned his human hands into claws that ripped and teeth that tore.

He remembered swallowing the blood of the human to feed Roman with pain and suffering.

He remembered standing over his kill and panting with excitement and gleeful satisfaction.

He remembered licking his fingers clean as if they had been covered in the sweetest of candy.

He remembered watching the blood disappear from his clothes and body, before walking back to his pickup and driving off as if nothing had happened. Singing to the radio and keeping time to the beat of the drums with his head carried him all the way home until he pulled in his yard and saw the Guardians there waiting for him.

Wyatt remembered it all.

And felt nothing.

"Good boy!" Roman said.

"Good boy!"

Chapter 62

Ethan walked up to the Sheriff and laid a hand on his back in support.

"Hey Ethan," the head of the police said in a tired voice. "Guess I don't have to ask what brings you here, do I?"

"I heard so I came. I thought I might be able to help. Don't know what I can do, but I'm here if you need anything. What happened?" Ethan asked with genuine concern.

Sheriff Hesper took the hat from his head and wiped the sweat from his brow.

Murder was an ugly affair and one that was almost unheard of in their small town. But he was standing over the proof that no one was safe from the hand of evil. Not even the children.

"It looks to be a young boy," Hesper said, telling Ethan what he knew. "Can't tell the who yet. That will have to wait for the coroner to figure out. It won't be long before some worried parent calls and reports their son didn't make it home from school today. Pretty sure that will give us a confirming ID. Bad shit here though," he said, shaking his head. "Bad shit!"

Ethan nodded his head and gave silent thanks that his son was standing beside him and it would not be him that got the worst call any parent could think of.

"What happened?" Ethan asked again.

"Looks like an animal attack," Hesper said, squaring his shoulders before angling to look Ethan in the eye.

"Rumor has it that you just took in a stray wolf recently," he said. "Care to tell me if you know where the animal was this afternoon?"

Ethan felt the back of his neck heat up with the unspoken accusation.

"Floyd was with me today until I went in the house," Ethan said, as he fought to keep the anger from his voice. "After I went in the house he stayed on the porch until I came out to come here. Why?"

"How do you know?" the Sheriff asked.

"Know what?" Ethan asked, making him spell it out for him.

"Know that he was on the porch? Know that he didn't do this? Where is he Ethan?" Hesper asked. It was his job to ask the hard questions, but he didn't have to like it.

Ethan turned to point to the back of his truck but Floyd was gone, vanished.

"He was in the back of my truck a minute ago," Ethan said baffled. "I don't see him now though."

Both men turned to scan the area but they found no Floyd.

Sam stepped up to Ethan and Hunter stood by the Sheriff. Each put their hand upon their human. Hunter pulled the suspicions Hesper harbored about Floyd from his mind and planted an unshakable belief that the wolf had done no wrong.

Sam pulled the sick fear from Ethan until he was sure the mortal knew without a doubt that his wolf was innocent of any wrong doing.

Both Guardians calmed the humans before stepping back to continue to watch the drama unfold around the dead body.

They watched as sly glances were angled at Ethan and they heard the whispers of rumors starting to spread. Rumors that the wolf was responsible for the death they looked upon.

"We need more help," Jaxon said, having his hands already full as he worked to rid the onlookers of the thoughts in their heads.

Sam and Hunter lifted their heads and sent out a call for help. Within seconds the pasture was filled with Guardians until every human had a winged protector standing at their side.

They worked in silence until the sly glances and the angry whispers ceased.

"You know we can't tell them who really did this don't you?" Hannah said when her work was done. "There is no evidence that Wyatt was to blame and we can't just tell them either."

"So what are we to do now?" Dee asked.

"This will have to go down as one of the ones that will never be solved," Jaxon said, feeling frustrated at having to let the real culprit go free.

The Guardians moved until a circle was formed three deep around the boy and he had nowhere to go.

Wyatt showed no fear as Roman hunkered down inside him and whispered that he was safe.

That as long as he was with him, he was safe.

Safe from the Guardians that stood around him and tried to scare him with their show of force.

Roman gloated until the circle of his enemies parted and Omega stepped inside. When the circle closed again Roman gloated no more as he looked upon the Beast. Not only the Beast, but the Guardian that burned with fire at his side.

Ashton and Omega had come to play and they were not going to leave until Wyatt lay at their feet and Roman was put to death.

Roman quaked, but he was not done yet.

He sent out a call of his own.

He called for help.

He called for Saul.

Chapter 63

Saul came.

He came with thunder.

He came with lightning.

He came with wind.

He came with a crash.

The circle of Guardians parted to let him pass before, once again closing ranks behind him, trapping the human and his cargo.

"How dare you call me!" Saul said, anger dripping from his words. "I do not come at your whim!" he spit out.

"But you do come for this soul," Roman said, speaking so no human ear could hear.

"It would seem that your followers are ready to do battle and the first victim will be this boy!" the Dark One promised. "How do you like that?"

Saul was torn between wanting to save Leonard's soul and wanting to drive out Roman, until he could get his hands around the Dark wraith and turn him to ash.

"Explain!" Saul said, waiting for one of his close friends to speak up.

"Wyatt has committed murder," Jaxon said, stepping to Saul's side. "With the help of the filth that leeches inside him he has taken an innocent life. He must pay!"

Saul looked upon the ruined body of the once human and he felt sorrow and pity for the boy that would not grow to be a man.

"Not only that," Omega growled "but he has now placed fear in the hearts of the mortals that stand and look upon this deed. They will take up their guns and hunt the ones with claws and fangs until they are erased from this land. They will hunt those that are innocent of this deed because of this human and his master. They will hunt the ones I protect!"

Omega looked into Saul's eyes and his own burned with anger.

"I will not allow this!" the Beast growled. "I will not allow the ones I protect to be slaughtered for a crime they did not commit."

Omega turned his fiery eyes from Saul until they rested on Wyatt and Roman. He took a step closer and bunched his muscles, preparing to attack.

But he did not leap, as Saul stepped between the boy and the Leader of all Animals.

"Get out of my way!" the Beast commanded the mightiest Guardian of them all. "Get out of my way or fall with the boy!"

But Saul did not move.

He stood tall and unfurled wings of the purest white until Wyatt was taken from the Beast's sight.

"A human life was taken here," the Immortal said, his voice ringing out with strength and power. "Since it is a human life that needs to be avenged the Guardians will be the ones to hand down the justice for this deed."

"It was not the boy that took a life, but the Dark One that clings to him," Saul reasoned.

"Wyatt allowed it," Alpha said, stepping into the circle to join her mate. "He allowed Roman into his mind, his body, and his soul. He allows this and he likes the power the Dark One gives him. He is now evil and must be put down."

Saul faced the pair of Beasts but he did not fear them. He felt their anger at the threat that was now placed upon the ones they protected and he could not fault them for their actions.

"My Guardians and I will take care of the minds of those here until the thoughts of hunting are no more," Saul bargained with the Beasts.

The Guardians recognized an order when given and moved off to begin the process of changing the minds of the humans that had gathered.

"What of the rest of humanity?" Omega asked. "What about all the so called hunters that pick up a gun for a weekend of killing my kind?"

Saul hung his head as he had no answer for the Beast. He, better than anyone, knew that humanity was mean and liked to kill.

They killed for sport.

They killed because they cared not what they killed, just as long as they got to kill something.

When the taste for blood was fed by the Dark, they killed each other and that was okay with Omega. Better them than the ones he protected.

Omegas lips curled up in disgust as he could see that Saul had no answer for him. "Take away this threat!" he said. "Do it now and we will find a way to protect my innocents!" Omega said, knowing he was defeated when it came to changing the human race.

"Everything that walks this Earth kills others for food," Saul reasoned, trying to ease the mind of his friend.

"Not all humans kill for food!" Alpha snarled before she began to whimper. She felt the pain of every animal that was killed for its fur or its feathers or merely for the fun of seeing it die.

Her heart broke with the shame of it all.

Omega supported her weight as she sagged with her grief.

"I will give you a few days. Maybe even a few weeks to decide what you will do to stop this soul before I step in," the Beast conceded, rising up to his full height.

Saul nodded his head and pulled his wings in close to his side.

"So be it," Saul agreed.

Omega and Alpha turned to leave the Guardians to do what they could.

Ashton had heard what was said and she followed the pair.

The wind began to rise as the two prepared to leave but died down again as Ashton approached and blocked their way.

"I have a plan," she said, for their ears alone.

They listened.

They smiled.

Chapter 64

Saul and his Guardians stayed until the last of the mortals had left.

Until the body of the boy was put in a black bag and driven away.

Until Ethan deemed there was no more he could do.

Until Wyatt, gloating along with Roman at having gotten away with murder, climbed into the truck with his father and headed home.

Until all was quiet except the wind blowing through the dead grass of late winter.

All was quiet.

"The time has come Saul," Jaxon said, receiving nods of agreement from Ashton, Sam, Hannah, Hunter and Dee.

"We need to put an end to this once and for all," Sam said, using a quiet voice to relay his concern. "We don't have a choice any more."

"Agreed," Saul said, silencing every other comment. "A life has been taken and we cannot let this action pass unavenged."

"Do you have a plan?" Ashton asked, interested in seeing if Saul's plan could play out with her own.

"Two weeks," Saul said.

"Two weeks what?" Hunter questioned for them all.

"In two weeks the moon will be full and I intend to confront Roman," Saul enlightened them.

"Define confront," Ashton said, knowing that Wyatt had now gotten a taste of killing and Roman was going to feed that hunger until it became a raging inferno.

She had been inside Wyatt enough trying to clean the Dark from him that she knew the boy better than he knew himself.

She knew his soul.

"A fight," Saul said, making the others take a step closer to him in interest.

"A fight?" Dee asked, not liking the sound of this.

"To the death," Saul continued, preparing to lay out his plan.

"I am going to challenge Roman to a fight over Leonard's soul. Only one of us will walk away," Saul concluded.

"How will you get him to leave the boy?" Jaxon asked, seeing a major flaw in Saul's plan.

"Do you really think Roman will be able to resist a challenge from me?" Saul asked. "He will be jumping at the chance to finally pit himself against me. His ego will not let him turn down the chance to defeat me in battle."

"And when are you going to issue this invitation to Roman?" Sam asked, his mind recalling his mortal profession. He knew what it took to prepare for a killing.

"Not until the night of the full moon," Saul said. "I will give him no time to plan or to call up his Dark Ones to cover his back. It will seem a spur of the moment thing and the deed will be done."

"I will leave it up to you," Saul said, turning to Jaxon "to get the boy here when it is time."

"Right here?" Jaxon asked, wanting clarification.

Saul let his eyes wander over the few trees and the grassy expanse before looking back at Jaxon.

"Right here." Saul restated. "There are few objects here in which Roman's followers can hide. The full moon will show us any that approach and it will be up to you to keep them back, from trying to aide their leader."

"We have a couple of weeks to work all the kinks out," Jaxon said to the others in the group.

"Very well! We will do as you ask," Jaxon said, turning to Saul and giving him all of their support.

Saul nodded his head and opened his wings to fly.

"Where are you going?" Dee asked, thinking they would all stay together and talk strategy.

"I will take this time and prepare myself for the battle," Saul said, meeting each of their eyes in turn.

Saul cared for all the Guardians in his care but these six were close to his heart and he would move heaven and hell to protect them. He wondered if they knew this.

"We will see you here in two weeks time," Sam said, allowing Saul to leave as he wanted.

"But can he win?" Dee asked into the silence that followed Saul's departure.

No one answered.

Chapter 65

The Guardians may have had a plan, but so did Roman. He did not know what was coming but he was far from stupid. He knew his enemies would not allow him to unleash Wyatt on mankind to kill at will.

It would take some cunning on his part to shake the ones set to guard his puppet as they tried to protect their innocent charges. A pain to be sure but not insurmountable.

Really they should be thanking him, Roman reasoned for he, at first, only planned to cull the ones that were weak and useless. Wyatt was far from experienced and must be given the easy ones until he was confident and hungered for more of a challenge.

Roman rubbed his hands together in anticipation of the blood he and Wyatt were about to spill.

Roman allowed Wyatt to see the blood that would flow and feel the power that came with taking a pitiful human life. The boy's reaction was all he could hope for, as he itched to be set free. Free to kill again and again and again, until his belly and soul were filled to bursting.

Roman knew the feelings that coursed through Wyatt. He knew Wyatt had tasted the power and wanted more. Much more.

Roman would set the table for his human and feast along side him as they both dined on the fear and pain inflicted, before allowing their chosen victim to die.

Dust off their hands, wipe their lips and move on to the next.

Roman could not wait.

The hunger for chaos and death grew until it spilled over into Wyatt.

Both became restless.

Both became hungry.

Both became the hunter.

Both became death.

Chapter 66

Sam stood over the torn apart body of the mortal child as his anger grew, turning him cold and deadly.

He knew this was Wyatt's doing. Wyatt's and Roman's. As vigilant as the Guardians had become, Roman had succeeded in claiming a life. An innocent life.

Sam was angry!

For a week the Guardians had stayed close to Wyatt keeping an eye on him. Letting Roman and Wyatt see them. Never hiding their intentions, thinking that if the Dark knew they were being watched they would lay low and wait for an opening that would not come before striking down another mortal.

They were wrong.

Roman had been busy sending out his followers to cause chaos. Laughing to himself as mankind tore at each other and wars were started. He knew the Guardians would have their hands full, trying to undo the havoc he was responsible for.

He was not wrong. Add one to the win column for the Dark. Roman's plan was working perfectly.

The Guardians had had to peel off from guard duty to repair the damage and while they were away Wyatt had been busy.

More innocent mortals had been ripped to shreds, leaving wails of despair from loved ones mounting until Roman danced in glee. Their cries really were music to his ears.

Wyatt fell in love with the act of murder and he thought of nothing else.

He watched with eyes of lifeless black as his classmates, his once friends and even his father went about their pointless lives, never knowing that he plotted each of their deaths.

Wyatt stood over his father as he slept, night after night, trying to figure out a way to tear his flesh until he was nothing but a pile of gore. How to do it without the blame falling on him was the only reason his father still drew breath.

Oh yes, the only reason Ethan had been spared his son's new passion was that the boy was still trying to work out the details.

"Why do you think so hard on this matter?" Roman asked, bored with the way Wyatt hesitated. "Just do it and be done."

Wyatt still hesitated.

"But he is my father," the boy said, a tiny spark of goodness staying his hand.

"I am your father!" Roman shouted, making Wyatt whimper in pain from the voice in his head. He was not used to Roman criticizing him. Up until now he had received only praise from the one living inside his body.

"Have I not remade you into something to be feared?" the Dark Master asked. "Have I not earned the love and respect one gives to a father?" the voice berated. "Have I not allowed you to become what you are today? Given you free rein to go out on your own and do what you love? Haven't I?"

"Yes," Wyatt answered, tears of pain and gratitude dripping down his cheeks. "Yes!"

"Then do this so we may move on. I will protect you as always. Kill him!" Roman screeched in a voice that grated like nails on a chalk board.

Wyatt raised his hand and watched as the nails grew long and sharp, just waiting for him to swing out with a blow that would cut through flesh like a hot knife through butter.

His hand trembled, but only for a moment as the one seed of goodness that remained was crushed under Roman's foot. The transformation was complete.

Wyatt felt nothing as he looked from his hand to the sleeping man on the bed.

He pulled his arm back to strike but before the motion was completed the hand, with its death dealing claws, was arrested in mid air.

Wyatt looked over his shoulder and hissed in hatred.

Sam stood in all his Immortal glory, gripping the hand that meant to kill Ethan.

Wyatt whirled and tried to rip his arm from the hand that held it but he could not. Sam held him fast.

"Get out!" Sam said, his voice cold as ice. "Unless you want to be the one to die this night I would suggest you get out. NOW!"

Sam wanted nothing more than to pick the boy up with a hand around his neck and hold him there until the air he needed was gone from his lungs.

He wanted to hear and feel the bones snap and watch as the life drained from the eyes that were as black as sin.

He wanted to end this madness so badly he could taste the bitterness of his want upon his tongue.

But he would not, could not, so he did the only thing he could and let the boy go.

Roman had a good laugh at what he thought of as weakness of the Guardian standing with them. He knew Saul would not let them take this life and he poked the bear with a stick of sarcasm.

"Well, well, well," he sing-songed through Wyatt. "If it isn't the big bad assassin. Not so big and bad now are we? Saul has you trained like a little bitch, afraid to do what is needed. How does it feel to be weak?" Roman asked, feeling invincible in his human suit.

"If you harm this man I will forget why we are not to kill you and be done with it!" Sam said, not letting the taunts Roman dished out bother him, even though the killer in him crept just beneath his skin wanting to escape. Just this once.

Roman had Wyatt bow to his enemy and laughed as he directed him to exit the room.

"Don't go far!" Roman threw over Wyatt's shoulder as they stood in the doorway. "Next time you may be too late." Still laughing, the son and his passenger left the room to Sam and his charge.

Sam did the only thing he could do.

He stayed.

He protected.

He burned, with the fires of anger, he burned!

He planned!

He hated!

Chapter 67

Sam stayed with Ethan until the last dust had settled from the departing Wyatt. Only then did he let out a tired breath and relax his shoulders. The urge to do harm quieted and the Immortal enjoyed the first peace he had had in a while.

"Hey Sam," Callie said, as she came down from a tree branch she had been sitting on.

"Hello Callie," Sam said, reaching down and allowing the little one to jump upon his shoulder. "I didn't know you were still around," Sam admitted, listening to the calming purrs rumble in his ear.

"I never left," the wee Guardian admitted. "I had to keep an eye on Ethan."

Sam nodded his head in agreement as his eyes once more stared off in the direction Wyatt had taken.

"I have something to show you," Callie said, landing at Sam's feet before leading the way towards the barn.

Sam followed and hoped, with all his heart, he was not going to find the dead body of an animal tossed into the dried bushes lining the back side of the barn. He wouldn't put it past Wyatt and his cohort to hurt or kill anything they could get their dirty hands on, be it human or animal.

Callie danced ahead and her fluffy tail wagged with each step she took. When she disappeared around the corner of the big barn Sam quickened his pace to catch up.

Rounding the corner Sam stopped short as he came face to face with Alpha and Omega as they stood side by side in his path.

Arching a handsome brow Sam looked at Callie for an explanation.

"Alpha and Omega wanted to talk to you," the wee one piped up.

Sam nodded his head once and again faced the beautiful pair of Immoral Wolves.

"What can I do for you?" he asked, curious as to why the meeting had to take place behind a barn.

"We have a gift for Ethan," Alpha said, happiness gleaming from her eyes.

Sam waited as Omega stepped aside and lowered his head. He dug deep into a pile of weeds before reemerging with a mouth full of brown and white fluff.

Sam waited as the Beast walked to him and looked him in the eye before opening his jaws to let the puff of fur drop into his waiting hands.

Sam's heart melted as a pair of soft brown eyes looked at him with total trust. The small mouth opened as the pup yawned before curling in a fluffy ball and settled down to close its eyes and sleep. It did not fear the Guardian that brought it to its chest and cuddled it there.

Looking at Omega, Sam waited for the Leader of Beasts to speak.

"This one needs a home," Omega said "and Ethan needs something to fill his heart with love and companionship. They will be a perfect match."

"I, we, are trusting you to introduce them and to keep this little one safe from the boy until Saul can put an end to this evil that has come to Ethan's house," the wolf said.

Sam stroked the soft fur as the pup slept and couldn't resist the urge to raise it to his face and place a gentle kiss upon the tiny head.

"Done," he said, as he turned to head to the house and the puppy's new home.

"Just one thing, a word of warning," Omega stopped Sam before he would walk away.

Sam looked back over his shoulder and, seeing the hard look in the silver eyes, he turned back with his innocent cargo but he already knew what was to be said.

"Should you fail in keeping this tiny one safe, it will give me great pleasure to taste the blood of the one who harms it," the Immortal Beast growled out.

"I and my kind will not wait for Saul to end Roman and his human. We will do it for him. This is a promise I make to you," Omega said, as the hair on his back stood up in a fierce line and his muscles rippled with power.

Sam had not a second's doubt as he knew the truth of what the Beast said.

Alpha and Omega watched over the ones that asked for nothing more than the love and kindness their keepers could and should provide.

"I know what you've done," Omega said. "I've seen what justice you have dealt out when you have come across abuse to one of mine. This is why I have entrusted this task to you. Do not fail me. Do not fail this little one."

"Callie and I will watch over this one," Sam said, looking for confirmation from the small Guardian at his feet.

Callie purred in agreement. "I will stay with my new friend and warn Sam and the others if danger or harm is eminent," she said with all seriousness. "I swear!"

"Very well," Omega said, accepting their oaths to protect the pup. "I know I am putting this one in a dangerous place, but Ethan is in need of love and this one can give it to him with out reservation."

"It will give him peace now and for many years to come," Omega vowed knowing this to be true.

"Thank you," Sam said, as he turned again to leave.

Callie nodded her head to Alpha and Omega before following Sam's lead. She had a new charge and she wanted to be there when Ethan and his new friend were introduced.

She was happy.

Chapter 68

Ethan sat alone in his house with nothing to keep him company except the T. V. that was turned on for nothing more than noise.

Wyatt had gone out for the evening with barely a grunt to his father as he had shut the door behind him on his way into town.

The son that Ethan had raised on his own was nothing more than a stranger these days and Ethan felt the loss of their closeness deeply.

Day after day, night after night he wondered where he had gone wrong with his son.

His memories of the boy that clung to his legs and wanted to be near him always were just that, memories. Nothing more.

Ethan ran a tired hand through his dark hair that had begun to show white at his temples until it dropped to his side and lay still.

The sun was dipping into the west, leaving long shadows in its wake, but Ethan did not notice. He was just too tired to care.

He knew he should get up and make something to eat but he just didn't feel like it. He was sad. He was beaten.

Sam and Callie walked to the front door with their small package before Sam lay the pup down and went to find Ethan.

Sam stood and watched as Ethan's shoulders slumped and he felt the feelings of defeat from the father as if they were his own.

Laying a hand upon the mortal's shoulder, Sam took those feelings away until Ethan could draw a breath that was not filled with pain and sorrow.

"Go to the door," Sam whispered into the waiting ear. "Open it up."

Ethan's head came up and he cocked it to one side as if listening to something. He rose to his feet and went to the door, opening it and looking out into the deepening dark.

A small whimper made him look down and his eyes opened wide at the gift on his stoop.

"Where did you come from?" he asked, as he bent down and picked up the tiny warm body.

A small tongue came out and licked at the hand that held him before he was brought to a wide chest and a strong heart beat thumped in his ears.

Ethan held the pup away from him long enough to check out whether it was a boy or a girl before snuggling it under his chin and taking it inside.

"Let's go inside boy," he said, his heart feeling the first touches of love. "I think we need to find you something to eat, don't you?" He was rewarded with a vigorously wagging tail that made the little body shake with delight.

Sam and Callie watched as Ethan warmed up some leftovers and turned them to mush before setting the small dish down and placing the puppy before it.

The tiny wet nose sniffed before a small bite was taken. Ethan chuckled as tiny bites became bigger ones and small furry front feet ended up in the dish with the food. Another small dish was set out with warm milk and it was devoured. It wasn't long before a full belly had the pup sitting down in satisfaction.

Ethan couldn't resist as he picked up the puppy and held him close.

"Would you like to stay with me?" he asked the now sleepy bundle in his arms.

Velvety eyes opened wide and a wet tongue again licked him, as Ethan found a place in his heart for this tiny being and the puppy chose Ethan as his own.

"Well now, if you're going to stay, we will have to find a good name for you won't we?" Ethan asked the little one in his hands. "Let's get a good look at you and see what comes to mind."

He held the pup up until he was eye level with him and took a good look.

Snowy white hair covered his feet and round belly, with a rich dark brown saddle across and down his back. The same dark brown hair covered his head except for a white stripe that ran from between his eyes, down his nose and graced the underside of his chin and neck. His ears were rich velvety brown, all but the tips, which again were the blazing white, leaving only the tail to be examined.

Ethan had to smile as his perusal of that tail was an exercise in motion, as it seemed to be ever wagging and never still for more than a second at a time.

Nothing about the pup told him what kind of dog he was so Ethan assumed he was a mixed breed and he didn't care.

Not being able to help himself, he brought the dog, his dog, back to his chest and bent his head to place a kiss on the oh so soft head. A tear came to his eyes as he held on for dear life to the one thing that would love him no matter what. He needed that! He needed a friend.

"How about we call you Buddy?" he asked the now yawning puppy. "I think I need a buddy and you will fit the bill just fine."

Buddy looked up at him and wagged his tail, as if to say he agreed with his new name.

Ethan laughed and headed for the door.

"We might as well start you off right," he said, taking Buddy out to the yard and setting him down on the edge of the grass.

"Time to do your business," Ethan said, hoping Buddy would get the idea of what was expected of him.

Callie whispered into the little one's ear and explained what he was expected to do before standing back and letting him get to it.

Ethan grinned as Buddy took care of what he was to do. Not just one but both and he was sure he had a smart dog on his hands.

"Good boy," Ethan said when Buddy came to him and wanted to be picked up. He obliged him and praised him over and over again, letting his new friend know he had done well.

Ethan knew it was a bad idea, but for this one night he let the puppy sleep with him in his bed.

For the first time in a long time Ethan fell asleep happy.

Happy and loved.

Callie and Sam smiled.

Chapter 69

Wyatt did not get home until the wee hours of the morning. He made noise, slamming the door and stomping his way up the stairs until he reached his room and closed the door behind him with a bang.

He didn't care if he woke Ethan up or not.

"Why don't you do it now?" Roman asked, an ever dark voice in Wyatt's head. "Just go into his room and do it. It's time!"

Without hesitation, Wyatt walked back out of his room and stood before the closed door that hid his father from his eyes.

He reached out a hand to turn the door knob and saw his hands turn to the now familiar claws of death. The black, broken nails, that cut and tore human and animal flesh alike, had become his tools. He used them until the hunger that lay in his belly was satisfied and, for a time quiet.

He felt that hunger rise up now and gnaw at him until he thought of nothing else except feeding it on demand. It, Roman, demanded a meal now.

The knob turned with no sound and Wyatt swung the door wide before moving to stand at the side of the bed where Ethan lay sleeping on his side. His back was to Wyatt and, as much as Wyatt would have liked to see his father's eyes when he tore into him, he settled for attacking him from behind.

Wyatt raised his arm above his head and prepared to strike, but stopped as a strange sound reached his ears.

A tiny growl of warning came from the bed before a small, furry body peeked its head over Ethan and stared at the boy.

Wyatt smirked before licking his lips and drooling in anticipation.

"Oh look," Roman crowed. "We have a before meal snack," the Dark One said with glee. "Must be an appetizer. Yummy!" he said, before directing Wyatt to dispatch the small one first.

Wyatt reached out a filthy hand, but before he could snatch Buddy up, pain shot up his arm and Roman cried out in warning. He was too late.

That same filthy hand was now in the jaws of a Beast, and not just any Beast, but Omega himself.

Omega knew, without a doubt, he would be needed so he had stayed close until the mortal one called him. Called him with a tiny growl of a puppy, but backed by the courage of a wolf.

Omega answered that call.

Eyes of silver shone bright as Omega locked them on his prey and bit down just a little harder, until his long teeth felt the fragile bones of the human boy.

He wanted to snap those bones until Roman and Wyatt screamed in pain, but he held back just short of his desire.

Time drug on before, ever so slowly, the strong jaws opened, allowing Wyatt to snatch his hand back and he cradled the injury against his chest with a whimper.

"Get out!" Omega growled, low and deep. "Get out and never let me catch either of you trying to hurt this one again. Should you not heed my warning and come for him again, I will kill you. Slowly and with much pain, I will kill you! This is your one and only warning. Now get out!"

"You can't kill us," Roman said, certainty in the voice that reached Omega's ears. "Saul and the Guardians won't allow it."

"Go ahead!" Ashton said, appearing at Omega's side. "Do it!" she urged the Beast.

And Omega wanted to. He wanted to taste the blood of the mortal standing before him until he almost panted with the need.

"This isn't over!" Roman screamed, as he retreated with Wyatt from the room. "You can't watch all the time and, when you are gone, we will strike. This isn't over!" he screamed again, before the closing of the door to Wyatt's room cut him off.

Omega lifted his muzzle to the sky and howled out his frustration.

Ashton stood by his side until the last notes died away and the Beast shook himself from head to toe.

"How long?" Omega asked, looking to Ashton for an answer. "How long until Saul finishes this?"

Ashton moved to the window and looked up into the sky that was just now beginning to show the first signs of a new day.

She spied the moon and gave him an answer.

"Two days." she said. "Two days until we end this."

Omega curled his lip and a low growl rumbled in his chest.

"Very well," Omega conceded. "Saul has two days. You may tell him that after that I will take care of it for him."

Omega stooped to nuzzle the small puppy that had, once again, curled up beside his human, letting him know that he had done a good job.

Buddy rubbed his head against the Immortal's muzzle before closing his eyes to sleep once more.

"Two days," Omega said, one more time to Ashton. "Two days and then I come back." With a gust of wind he was gone, leaving Ashton to stand guard alone.

As she watched over the two beings in the bed, small flames danced over her hands and licked up her arms. Her desire for an ending was no less than Omega's.

"Two days," she repeated. "Two short days before I wait no longer." After that she would be by Omega's side and the plan she had come up with, should Saul fail, would be set into motion.

She smiled with eyes half closed and lips curled up in anticipation.

She smiled.

Chapter 70

Ethan woke this morning later than usual. The sun had already broken the horizon, but for once he stayed in bed just a few minutes longer.

He probably would have stayed asleep longer too, but a cold nose had nudged his cheek and a wet tongue had showered him with puppy kisses.

"Hi Buddy," Ethan said, smiling as he gathered the wiggling bundle to him. "I bet you have to go outside, don't you?"

Ethan hurriedly pulled on his clothes, while keeping an eye on the bundle of energy that was bouncing on his bed. Scooping him up, he headed down the stairs and out the door just in time, as Buddy squatted immediately and, when finished, earned himself more praises and good boys for his deed.

The next order of business was to find Buddy something to eat.

Ethan stood in front of his refrigerator trying to find something for his new companion. He obviously didn't have any puppy food so he was going to have to be creative until he could make a quick trip into town.

He was just finishing cooking an egg for Buddy when the sound of heavy foot steps announced the arrival of his son into the kitchen. Turning with the dish that held the egg and a small patty of left over sausage, Ethan met his son's eyes.

"Morning," he said with a smile, trying to be cheerful and upbeat as he greeted Wyatt as he set the dish down for Buddy.

"What's that?" Wyatt asked, pointing an accusing finger at the dog chowing down at Ethan's feet.

"I found him on the porch outside the back door last night," Ethan started to explain. "I think we have a new puppy and I named him Buddy. What do you think?"

"About what?" Wyatt asked, as he stepped around the two to get some juice out of the fridge.

"About the new puppy. About his name. About anything?" Ethan said, recognizing the tone of his son's voice and feeling the tiredness creep over him once more. He didn't want to fight. He just wanted them to be a happy family again and together, be happy with the newest member to their family.

Sam stood by Ethan's side and took the feelings away until Ethan could once more find joy in his new companion.

Ethan pulled out the chair closest to his dog and sat down to eat a bowl of cereal before starting his chores.

"You want something to eat?" Ethan offer as he pointed to his bowl, willing to get up and make a quick breakfast for his son.

"I'll get it myself," Wyatt groused, barely missing the puppy as he stepped around him.

Buddy ate with enthusiasm, but kept a close watch on the boy with eyes that showed white and ears that lay flat against his tiny head.

"Be careful," Roman warned his host. "This one has powerful friends," and he let Wyatt see Sam as the Guardian lounged against the cupboard with arms crossed over his wide chest.

"Feeling froggy?" Sam asked Wyatt, as he knew what the boy was thinking. "Go ahead and jump then!" the Immortal dared.

Wyatt lifted his middle finger up and waved it in Sam's direction, making the Guardian chuckle, not in the least bit intimidated.

Ethan finished his meal and placed both his and Buddy's dishes in the sink before heading into the bathroom to get ready to do the chores.

The minute he was out of sight Wyatt came to his feet and reached out his hands to grab the puppy.

"Don't!" Sam warned, as he crouched with wings unfurled and prepared to do battle.

Callie came to Buddy's side and hissed a warning, as her hair stood on end and her fangs grew long.

"Remember last night?" Roman hissed, looking to see if Omega was going to appear again.

Wyatt stopped and rubbed the arm that Roman had had to heal, as he indeed remembered the deep teeth marks that had caused him such pain.

"Damn dogs!" Wyatt muttered, just as Ethan entered the kitchen again.

"What's that?" Ethan questioned, thinking that Wyatt might actually be talking to him for once.

"Nothing," the boy mumbled, before plastering a smile on his face and throwing out an idea he came up with.

"How about you leave Buddy here with me while you do the chores? We can get to know each other," Wyatt said, all nice and sweet.

Ethan might have agreed if it had not been for Sam telling him to take the pup with him.

"Maybe later," Ethan said, as he scooped Buddy into his arms and carried him to the door, not sure why he had an uneasy feeling about leaving the two alone together.

The smile fell from Wyatt's face and he glared at his father's back until the door closed behind him.

"I told you to be careful," Roman scolded, but Wyatt was in no mood to listen as his belly rumbled and his mouth went dry.

The hunger was growing and cereal was not going to satisfy it.

Wyatt went to the fridge and opened the door, taking out a pack of thawed steaks that Ethan was planning on bar-b-cueing later. He ripped open the package and brought the meat to his face, breathing deeply as the scent of the blood dripping down his hands made his mouth drool.

Wyatt chewed and tore and gnawed on the flesh until it was devoured in big chunks, easing his hunger as he filled his belly.

Roman smacked his lips as, he too, tasted the raw meat and the blood that it lay in.

Wyatt let out a big burp of satisfaction before heading to the sink to clean his bloody hands.

With his hands under the water, Wyatt's actions slowed until he stopped scrubbing and stood staring out the window with eyes of black.

He watched as his father walked towards the house with Buddy, his new best friend, galloping on his short legs, trying to keep up.

He watched as Ethan bent down and lifted the small dog, sparing him the effort of running behind him.

He watched as his father petted the dog and planted a kiss on his head, smiling and happy, before they both came up the steps and he heard the door open and close.

His belly rumbled.

He was hungry again.

Chapter 71

Wyatt spent the day in his room, but Ethan didn't care. He went about his day with Buddy at his side and he was happy.

The day grew warm, as a hint of spring was in the air, chasing away the bitter cold of winter and giving way to the promise of new beginnings just around the corner.

Ethan whistled while he worked and Buddy was happy to dance around his feet and be a part of what turned out to be a really good day for both man and his dog.

The bond between the two was formed and cemented before the sun dipped into the west and a million stars came out to light the night sky.

Ethan took Buddy out one more time and stood looking at the nearly full moon while his new pal did his business before calling it a night.

"It's going to be a full moon tomorrow night," Ethan told the dog, as he let him romp one more time around the yard.

"Time goes so fast," Ethan continued, talking as if there was someone to listen to him. And indeed there was, as Buddy came to sit at his feet and stare up into the night sky with his human.

Buddy didn't know what Ethan was saying, but he liked the tone of his voice and he knew his master was happy too.

"Take him inside now," Callie whispered to her charge, as the shadows began to creep with the Dark. "Stay with him again tonight and keep him safe. Call if you need me and I will come."

Buddy whimpered in agreement, drawing Ethan's attention.

"Okay Buddy, let's go inside," Ethan said, picking up the little bundle and heading in for the evening.

Wyatt was nowhere to be seen. So Ethan locked the doors and mounted the stairs, telling himself again that one more night with Buddy sharing his bed was not going to hurt anything.

The light went out and the house grew still, as both man and his dog slid into peaceful sleep, neither one aware that they had protectors watching over them. Keeping them safe.

For one more night they would keep them safe.

After that everything would change.

For better or for worse, everything was going to change.

Chapter 72

The night passed without incident and Ethan woke the next morning well rested, and again felt happy, as Buddy licked his face in greeting and love.

"Well good morning to you too," Ethan said, as he turned his face this way and that, trying to avoid the happy tongue that was hell bent on giving him a bath.

Ethan thought it best not to linger, as he was sure Buddy probably had to pee, and since he was doing so well in that area, he did not want to give his new friend the chance to back slide even once.

Jumping out of bed, Ethan hurried and dressed before scooping up the waiting puppy and made a mad dash down the stairs and out the door to the far grass they had been using.

Setting him on his feet, Ethan backed up to give him some space and was once again delighted that Buddy knew just what to do.

"You are one smart dog," he praised, giving the soft coat a good brushing and a few pats of his hand. Buddy wiggled and tried to lunge for the face so close to his to give it some loving in return.

The smile on Ethan's face slipped a little as they entered the house together and found Wyatt sitting at the table with his normal sullen expression riding his face.

"Do you want some breakfast before school?" the father asked, trying to make small talk and get his son to talk in return.

Before Wyatt could answer, his stomach gave a lengthy growl and Ethan took it as a sign that he did want something to eat.

"I'll get something on the way to school," Wyatt said, gathering his backpack and slinging it over his shoulder.

"You got money?" his father asked, trying to make sure he had enough to get something besides a donut and a drink.

"I guess I could use a few bucks. I have something going on after school today and won't be home for supper," Wyatt said, hating to have to take anything from his father. His human father.

Ethan set Buddy down and reached in his back pocket for his wallet. He pulled out a couple of twenties and held them out for Wyatt to accept.

Wyatt did so without a thank you and stuffed them in his jeans pocket before turning to leave.

"You know I still love you, don't you?" Ethan asked, wanting badly to put his arms around his son and squeeze him tight.

"Sure Dad," Wyatt said, his heart cold and unmoved by his father's declaration. "See ya." And he left without a backward glance.

Ethan didn't know why, but he had the feeling he should go after him and not let him go until they had talked about whatever it was that had turned Wyatt into the angry young man that he now was.

Ethan stepped out onto the porch, but he was too late. Wyatt gunned the motor of his pickup and left the yard in a cloud of dust.

"Bye Wyatt," Ethan said, lifting his hand in farewell. He shivered as he had the feeling that this really was good bye.

Buddy scratched at the door, drawing Ethan's attention to him. A small smile curved his lips as Ethan opened the door and scooped up his new friend.

"I guess it's just you and me today," he said, sighing in sadness.

Buddy would not let him stay sad for long, as he cuddled up to the warm chest with all the trust and love Ethan so badly needed now.

Ethan's heart grew large as the love he felt from his dog was returned a hundred fold.

"Come on Buddy," Ethan said, making the puppy wiggle in excitement. "Let's get our chores done so we can enjoy the rest of the day."

That sounded like a plan to Buddy. He was happy to skip and stumble along beside his master as they headed towards the barn and the cows that needed to be fed.

Both dug into their day, blissfully unaware of what changes were coming. Heading towards them like a runaway train was the Guardian's plan to either save Wyatt or kill him.

The outcome was still unclear.

They worked and played the day away until the shadows grew long and the sun gave way to the full bright moon.

Ethan had always felt drawn to the moon and had watched the bright orb in awe almost every night of his life.

Buddy shared his fascination and the two gazed up until the chill of the evening chased them inside.

Ethan remembered Wyatt telling him that he would be home late so he locked up the house he called home and climbed the stairs, bringing Buddy with him.

He had picked up a doggie bed in town and on this night he placed the articled on the top of his covers and lay the pup down on it.

Buddy seemed happy and snuggled down, only resting when Ethan joined him.

The lights went out, but the moon lit the bedroom as if they were still on.

All was quiet as the two slipped into restful sleep, not knowing what this night held for their family.

The moon knew.

The moon knew all secrets but it kept silent.

Still and silent.

Chapter 73

Saul stood before the Window to the World, trying to find the good in humanity. Trying to find a reason, besides the soul of Leonard, to fight the Leader of the Dark. Fight and win.

For two weeks he had watched the mortals, hunting for a spark to ignite the passion in himself, a will to fight once again. He was tired, so tired.

Since time began he had watched over mankind, helping to guide them and to fulfill the story that destiny had written for each and every one of them.

On this day, the day of the full moon, he stood one more time before the Window to the World, with shoulders that sagged and a heavy heart. He was hunting one last time for some piece of goodness left in the world.

As he searched he came upon a scene that made him pause and watch.

A small girl with dirty hair, dirty hands and torn clothes was playing in an open field beside a pile of rocks, because she had no toys to call her own. All alone, she played, carrying on a running conversation with her rocks and a ragged looking stick that she was using for a doll.

Saul's heart hurt for the ragged little girl, but as he continued to watch his reason to fight was born.

As the little one sat on the dry grass and played, it was not long before she was joined by a small rabbit and a lone fox. The fox did not hunt the rabbit and the rabbit did not fear its mortal enemy, but instead both had been drawn to the girl, drawn to her because of her love for animals of all kinds.

A smile grew on her dirty little face and she greeted both animals with joy and compassion.

Saul bent closer to the Window and watched as the girl pulled a meager sandwich from her pocket and carefully unwrap it. She broke off small pieces and held out her hands for each beast to take her offered gift and continued to do so until their bellies were full and sated, while her's remained empty.

Saul dared to look into her future and knew her destiny.

She would be blessed with the love of animals and would do great things for Omega and the ones he protected.

She would be happy and live a long life, filled with love and meaning.

Saul's faith in mankind was renewed as he watched one who had so little give all that she had to others to ease their plight, never thinking of herself. Never holding back.

If there were ones such as this innocent young girl still in this world, then Saul knew he would keep fighting to give them a chance at spreading the good they had inside.

If even one such soul, filled with goodness and innocence still existed, then Saul knew he and the Guardians would continue to fight the Dark, to give goodness a chance to survive and thrive.

He would fight for hope.

The Window grew dark as Saul stepped back. His shoulders no longer sagged and his muscles corded as he opened his mighty wings before throwing back his head. He roared!

He roared until the clouds at his feet turned black and boiled.

He roared until lightning flew with thick ropes of his rage, setting the sky on fire.

He roared until all who heard knew of his anger at mankind for being so weak that they willingly came to the table the Dark set for them. Feasting on the hate and greed and selfishness it offered, until they were ripe for the taking.

He had had enough.

It was time.

Time to fight.

Time to reclaim the humans and pull them back from the edge of Darkness.

He had had enough!

The moon smiled.

Chapter 74

Wyatt had lied to his father. He had nothing special to do after school, as he had claimed. He just didn't want to go home. He now hated the place he had shared and loved with his father for all his young life.

Now it was too boring. Roman had shown him what it was like to not be bored. He had shown him how to be feared and how to take what he wanted.

Wyatt liked it! He liked it all!

He liked walking down the halls of his school and having a wide path open for him. He liked seeing the fear in the eyes of his, once so called, friends and the teachers and everyone else. He liked the power fear gave him.

Roman did too.

Roman patted himself on the back often at being able to snatch one so special to Saul from under his nose and turn him so completely.

Damn he was good! Roman gloated.

Today the Leader of the Dark watched through Wyatt's eyes as the wind from the open window blew through the boy's curly, dark hair and dust flew from the dirt roads they traveled.

Roman whispered to Wyatt as he drove and laughed in glee as Wyatt did as he was told.

Nothing was safe, as the pickup flew into ditches and bounced over fields, tracking down animals and crushing them under the wide tires, until broken and dead bodies were left in a wake behind them.

Both laughed!

Roman was not stupid though. He kept a close watch to make sure Alpha and Omega did not surprise them and attack, as Omega had done a few nights before. He knew Omega would not hold back if he were to find out that his precious charges were being mowed down willy nilly by a human he had no liking for.

Roman would never admit to being afraid of the Beast, but deep in his shriveled little black heart lie the truth. The truth being that he was definitely afraid of the Beast and his followers.

They cared not who they harmed, only that vengeance was dished out in spades to the ones that abused or killed their charges.

It wasn't often that Roman got to have this kind of fun, but he felt safe as he knew Saul protected and fought for the one he now lived in. Omega was friends with Saul. So Roman let Wyatt loose to kill and maim whatever he wanted.

Ah, mortal life was grand! Wasn't it?

So Roman rode along as Wyatt bumped and bounced, hooting and hollering in encouragement, until the fading light made him quiet and take notice.

"It was early to be so dark," he mused, as he told Wyatt to slow the vehicle down and stick his head out the window.

"Wow!" Wyatt said, as he looked up at the angry clouds over his head. He climbed out to get a better view. "This looks bad. Maybe we should head home. Damn it!"

Wyatt's eyes turned black as Roman, too, looked up at the sky. But he had no intentions of going anywhere. He knew the reason for the storm that was brewing. "Saul must have his shorts in a bunch," he mused and giggled at his own use of words.

"Back in the truck!" Roman ordered, as he calmed Wyatt's fears of the brewing storm.

"Let's drive some more," Roman crowed, as he held on when the truck took off. "This is going to be a night to remember!" he told Wyatt and sighed in pleasure, as the boy agreed with him.

"A night to remember alright!" Roman repeated.

And he was going to enjoy every minute of it!

Chapter 75

Saul stood still, as one by one his friends joined him among the angry clouds. He waited until all six of them where there before turning to them and acknowledging their presence.

"Wasn't sure if this was your way of calling us all here, but we came anyway," Jaxon said, cocking an eyebrow at their leader.

Hannah, Dee and Ashton grouped together and also raised their eyebrows in question at Saul's appearance. Gone was the softer look portrayed by a polo shirt and slacks, once inspired by Sam. In its stead was the new look they were staring and wondering at.

Saul looked more like Jaxon, in his tight black tee shirt that showed off rippling muscles and toned rock hard abs. His pants had changed to black jeans that outlined his butt and the hard muscles in his long legs ending with black boots that looked mean and deadly.

"I guess good guys don't wear white any more," Hannah said, giving voice to their observations.

Saul glanced her way and snapped open his great wings of white. "Dressing in dark clothes will help even the odds tonight," he explained. "Only my wings will let Roman find me in the same dark he will try to hide in," Saul further stated.

"Smart move," Sam said, liking the changes Saul had made. "No use sticking out like a beacon in the dark when your opponent will blend in all too well."

Saul pulled his wings back in close to his body before taking a breath and began to speak.

"Before this night goes any further I need to thank all of you, my friends, for sticking by me against your better judgment," he said, letting his deep brown eyes linger on Ashton the longest.

"I have been lucky to call each and every one of you my friend," Saul said with sincere feeling.

"Whoa, whoa, whoa!" Hunter jumped in. "What's this 'have been' bull shit? There is no past tense here," he continued, his voice becoming louder with each word he uttered.

Saul smiled at him and reached out a hand until it rested on the broad shoulder.

"We all know I go to fight Roman tonight," Saul said, stating nothing but the facts. "And we all know the outcome of that meeting is far from a sure thing. For this reason alone I will say good bye to each one of you here and now so nothing is left unsaid."

"We don't need the words," Dee said, coming to Saul's side. She reached out a hand and touched Saul. She froze.

The gift of sight, past and future, that she had been born with as a human and carried with her as a Guardian, kicked in like a mule and she saw what was to happen.

Hunter went to her side and, putting his arm around her, pulled her away until she touched Saul no more.

"Don't tell me," Saul said, knowing what had just happened. "I don't want to know."

"Well I want to know!" Ashton said, stepping into the circle forming around Saul.

Dee turned her eyes to Ashton and shook her head no. "It is for Saul to decide, and if he says he does not want to know, then I will respect his wishes."

"Besides, what I see can change. It is not written in stone," Dee finished in a much softer tone of voice.

"Let it go," Sam said, not needing to be a mind reader to know what was to come might not be all they hoped for.

"We're here because you called," Sam said, as no one spoke to argue again. "What do you want from us?"

Saul looked from one set of Immortal eyes to another until his gaze had come full circle.

It had taken him eons as an Immortal Guardian to finally experience what humans had had all along. Friendship, family and love.

If Roman had really wanted to hurt Saul, all he would have had to do was hurt one of the six standing at his side, ready to do battle with him, for him and Roman would have had Saul at his feet.

Saul would do anything to protect his family. The thought of them in danger had the clouds boiling once more with his anger.

Sam, Ashton. Jaxon, Hannah, Hunter and Dee looked around them and wondered at the strength of the storm that sprang to life even more fierce than before.

Saul lowered his eyelids until they were mere slits and his chest rumbled with his feelings.

"Go get him!" Saul said to Sam, his voice deep and raspy.

"Go get Wyatt and meet me at the place of death. After that, don't interfere!" Saul said, not waiting for an answer before leaping into the air and disappearing.

"I'll get Wyatt there," Sam said, turning to the others. "After that we just have to stay out of sight and do as Saul said. Don't interfere."

Nods all around were received before Sam pushed off and went to find Wyatt and his parasite.

Ashton was the last to leave. She waited two heart beats before tipping her head to the sky and letting her call take flight.

"Omega!" she, whispered into the wind. "Omega it's time!"

Leaping to join the others, she listened to the wind and she heard it.

She heard the howl of the wolf, long and low and eerie. She had her answer.

Chapter 76

Wyatt drove with his window down, even though the skies rumbled with lightning and fierce clashes of thunder. The black clouds did their best to block out the full moon from his sight.

He didn't care. The power of the brewing storm did nothing but feed the hunger in him, until he drove with greater speed, hunting those that were weaker than him. Prey.

Roman too gained power from the darkness, as this was his element and he itched to taste it to its fullest.

"What's your hurry?" Sam asked, appearing in the passenger seat of the speeding truck.

Wyatt jerked the wheel and the truck rode on two wheels for a moment, until he got control before slamming on the brakes.

Turning his head to look at Sam, his deep blue eyes turned to flat black and the voice that spoke carried no human traits at all.

"Why have you come Guardian?" Romans voice poured out of the boy. "Be gone! You have no place here! Be gone before you force me to do something Saul will regret."

"I have something to show you first," Sam said, meaning to peak the Dark One's interest. And he did.

"Really?" Roman sneered. "What could you possibly have to show me that would interest me?"

"Meet me at the place where this human kills," Sam said, his voice hushed, as if sharing a secret.

"Why should I?" Roman asked, but he posed his question to the air as Sam had already disappeared.

Wyatt sat for a moment, drumming his fingers on the steering wheel, as Roman paced back and forth in his mind. He was thinking. Trying to decide what to do.

"What can it hurt?" Roman asked, without expecting a response from the only one who could hear him.

Maybe Sam was going to try to deal for the boy's soul. Maybe he was going to cross over to the Dark Side in exchange for this pet of Saul's. Or maybe he was just stupid enough to try something, trying to win Saul's favor. That's what his Minions would do.

What ever the reason, Roman could not deny his curiosity.

"Do we go?" Wyatt asked, feeling the first tingle of anticipation for the new adventure.

"Yes, yes we go," Roman said, creeping up close to the eyes he used as windows.

Roman watched as the few miles rolled by until he saw the meager stand of trees come into view. The same trees where Wyatt took his human victims and played with them until they could scream no more.

Wyatt pulled the pickup from the road until he parked it and shut off the motor. The only sound he could hear was the moaning of the wind, and with ever increasing frequency, the crack of the lightning as a fierce storm approached.

"I don't see anything," Wyatt said, not making a move to get out yet.

"Really?" Roman said with sarcasm. "Let's just go have a look see before you turn tail and run."

Stung by Roman's words, Wyatt swung the door open and got out before banging it closed in teenage anger.

"No need to be an asshole about it!" The boy said. He received a stabbing pain behind his eyes for his effort.

Roman laughed, but not for long, as the voice of his enemy spoke to him.

"Hello Roman," Saul said, as he stepped out into the open and faced the pair.

"What do you want?" Roman asked, his eyes darting everywhere at once, trying to see what lie in wait for him.

"I have come to challenge you for the boy's soul!" Saul said, not mincing words.

"I already have his soul!" Roman crowed. "Why should I fight you for what is already mine?"

"You would turn down the chance to maybe defeat me once and for all?" Saul taunted. "You would play the chicken and hide inside the boy instead of coming out and fighting as a leader should?"

"I don't know why you challenge me now!" Roman said, having Wyatt take one step back and then another, preparing to leave. "The only way you can make me come out is to kill the boy and we both know you won't do that. Don't we?" Roman asked, taking his turn at taunting his foe.

Saul could do nothing except watch as Wyatt and his cargo backed up one step at a time, until there were only a few feet left between him and the vehicle he would escape in.

His plan had not worked.

Lightning crashed beside Saul and when it vanished, Ashton stood there, dressed in black with her blood red wings unfurled and hands on fire.

Saul's plan may not have worked, but hers would not fail.

"NOW!" she commanded. "NOW!"

The wolf attacked.

Chapter 77

Omega had agreed to stay out of sight as Wyatt drove the dusty back roads out of town.

He had kept his word, but it was all he could do to restrain himself, as one after another of his charges were chased down and killed by the monster Saul was determined to save.

Tears of anger and pain rolled down his face, as he watched the spirits of those slain rise into the air and cross over to a better place where they would be cared for and know a life of happiness and love.

But with each spirit that rose, his anger grew until his muzzle dripped with his sorrow and his teeth ached to taste the flesh of the ones responsible.

Omega could not wait for Karma to open a path for him to seek revenge.

He took on Alphas role and became vengeance.

He watched as Sam did as instructed, and got his enemies to go to the place where Saul waited. But the plan fell apart, as Roman did not take the bait and come out to fight Saul.

Omega was glad!

He crouched down and waited until Ashton appeared and gave him the green light to attack.

And he did!

With one powerful bunching of pure muscle, the Beast leapt onto the human and, with ease, closed his jaws of death around his throat.

The momentum took the boy to the ground, and Omega squeezed until his screams of fright and pain were nothing more than gurgles of wetness.

Blood gushed into Omega's mouth and he let it run out, to spill upon the ground, turning the grass and dirt to deep dark red. It was tainted. He wanted none if it for his own.

He heard Roman scream in pain, but he did not let up. He cared not that his teeth had bit all the way through the mortal's neck and did not stop until, with a mighty shake of his head, he heard the snapping of bones like the breaking of twigs.

Only then did he drop the dead one at his feet and back up to await the exit of the Dark One.

Still Roman did not come out, but stayed crouched inside the body surrounded by the smell of blood and the stink of death.

"My turn!" Ashton said, as she walked up to stand beside the bloody Beast.

Falling to her knees, the Guardian placed hands that burned white hot with fire, onto the body and forced them inside, until Roman felt the heat of that fire and scrambled to escape it.

Dark smoke seeped from the mauled body, until Roman stood on his own for the first time in weeks.

He turned to flee but his escape was cut off, as the rest of Saul's friends formed a loose circle keeping Roman inside with Saul.

"You want a fight?" Roman ground out, spitting his words at Saul. "Very well then you shall have one. But it will be only you and I that fight this night!" he said, wanting to make sure he would not be jumped by the rest when he dispatched his hated enemy.

"Agreed!" Saul said, ruffling his wings as the full moon looked on. "No Guardian shall take my place if I should fall."

"Not if," Roman taunted, moving slowly around inside the circle. "But when. I should have done this ions ago."

"Come on then!" Saul urged "What are you waiting for? An invitation?" He laughed. He was tired of waiting and he could not look at Wyatt's body any longer.

He knew great sorrow, as he had watched the soul of Leonard leave the body and looked to him to save him once more.

Saul could not.

Not after all the death, pain and despair he had caused in this his last chance at life.

Saul stayed strong, as the ground opened up and Dark talons hooked Leonard's spirit and pulled it into the pit.

Saul closed his ears as Leonard begged him to save him, to give him one more chance.

Saul could not. Leonard's failures were on him, for he had been the one to allow him to be reborn.

Ashton had been right. He had been wrong.

It was over now. All but the fighting was over.

"I don't have all night!" Saul said, spreading his wings with their razor sharp edges and crouching slightly in preparation of Roman's attack.

"As you wish." the Dark One said smugly, and prepared himself for the battle.

As the Guardians and Beast watched, Roman grew until he stood as tall as Saul. His cracked and dirty nails became sharp as knives and his grey teeth were replaced by sharp pointed daggers.

Omega watched as the Guardians that formed the circle shifted in uncertainty. They had never seen this side of Roman before and he knew they worried for their friend.

Saul had said none of the Guardians would step in if he was to fall. That may have been true, but Saul did not speak for Omega and his kind.

Should Saul go down and Roman be the victor, Omega had every intention of ending him the same way as he had just taken Wyatt's life.

Not even the Dark could stand up to Alpha and Omega. He felt good knowing this was the last night Roman would walk this Earth and spread chaos and misery.

All he had to do was wait and watch.

Dark clouds rolled across the sky and in the blink of an eye Roman attacked.

Lightning crashed as the two Immortals came together and the Earth shook with their rage.

It had begun!

Epilogue

Saul rested on his hands and knees for a moment before trying to rise. His breath came in short, painful gasps, while his Immortal blood dripped and ran from the many cuts and gashes his battle with Roman had won him.

The beautiful, mammoth set of white wings were not so beautiful anymore. Many of their feathers now lay on the ground, surrounding him like new fallen snow. White no more, they were now stained with the black blood of the Dark One and the bright red that had been taken from Saul, as the Immortals had battled to the death.

Saul hung his head, as he tried to stand but could not. He was too tired, he was just too tired. He, ever so slowly, lowered himself until he lay on his side and remained there, giving a deep sigh and bringing his hands up until they made a pillow for his head. He stilled.

Saul opened his eyes, but could only see the moon. The massive bolts of lightning that had turned the night sky into day, only moments before, had died out when the Immortal battle had ended with Saul's victory.

The thunder that had rolled each time Roman and Saul had come together had faded until it was just a memory. The deep, ugly growl, that had struck terror in the hearts of the humans who had heard, was now silent and the blanket of peace was unfurled once more. Whatever had brought on the never before seen powerful storm had now passed them by.

The bright orb of the moon was blocked from Saul's sight as one by one his friends came to him. Sam and Ashton, Jaxon and Hannah and Hunter and Dee all rushed to surround their friend and leader that lay on the ground, broken and bloody.

"Take my hand!" Jaxon commanded, until a circle was formed around Saul. When the Guardians were linked, one by one they spread their wings, forming a feathery dome of power, concentrating as they tried to heal their fallen friend.

"More!" Jaxon ordered in desperation, "More!" A soft light grew until the sun paled in comparison with the healing power of the Immortal Guardians, as they joined together to try and close the open wounds that still ran red.

Jaxon's neck and arms corded with his efforts and, when he had no more to give, he threw back his head and roared until the earth shook and the heavens trembled.

The light slowly dimmed as one by one each had given every thing they had. Six pairs of great wings were folded until Saul was once more visible to all. But the wounds they had tried to heal were still raw and open. They had failed.

Six Immortal Guardians knelt by Saul's side, touching him, letting him know that he was not alone. Six Immortal

Guardians talked to him in soft voices, trying to sooth his pain, but Saul did not hear them.

All Saul heard was silence. He felt their hands and he felt their fear, but he heard nothing, as he lay on the ground and felt his breathing slow and, as it did, his pain subsided.

Saul's eyes opened to slits as the silence he had been drifting in was finally broken by a sweet voice that called his name.

"Saul!" it called, "Saul?"

"I can't help you any more" Saul said to the Fate that had appeared at his side. Its beauty shone from its being and Saul found peace as he looked upon that beauty.

"I have not come to ask for your help," the Fate said "but have come to give you what you have earned."

Saul turned his questioning eyes to his friends to see if any of them had an idea of what the Fate was talking about, but none seemed aware of the presence that had joined them.

"Since the beginning of time," the soothing voice explained, "you have been our champion, doing all that we have asked of you without question, without resentment. It is time Saul, time for you to join us."

"I don't understand" Saul whispered in his mind, "I don't understand."

"We are asking you to join us." the Being said. "We are asking you to be one of us. We are asking you to become a Fate."

Saul's mind registered the words spoken, but had a hard time grasping their meaning. He was to become a Fate?

The idea of not having to fight any more battles appealed to him and, as he weighed the pros of the offer, he began to smile.

Jaxon watched as a smile of pure peace grew on his friend's face and a coldness settled around his own heart.

"No!" Jaxon said, with growing sorrow. "Don't do this Saul! You have to fight and stay with us!"

"Not this time," Saul finally whispered. "My time here is over. Don't be sad for me," he counseled one more time. "I go to a better place and one day I pray that you will join me there too."

"Where?" Jaxon demanded. "Where are you going?"

Saul's soft brown eyes met Jaxon's one last time and he smiled before his now still form exploded into thousands of brilliant stars that scattered across the heavens, until each one had found a new home to shine down from. To watch over from.

Jaxon stared at his now empty hand and the Guardian Warrior joined his friends as they clung to each other and wept.

Omega lifted his muzzle into the air and wailed out the news and his sorrow to his kind. Alpha joined him and together they hung their heads to honor the fallen Guardian.

A gentle healing rain began to fall.

It rained yes, but the rain was made up of the tears from the Guardians.

There was no wailing or moaning or raging at the Fates to accompany the rain from above.

Only Silence.

It rained in silence!